THE **COOL BOFFIN**

'One of the funniest books I have ever read'
– Sunday Times

Pete Johnson says, 'When I was fourteen I changed schools and immediately became – invisible. I decided it was time for a new image. First of all I got a new hairstyle. Mum hated it, so I knew it was good. Then I bought some new clothes that I thought were cool . . . only they weren't at all. Years later I found one of those tragic shirts in the bottom of a drawer. I was taking in its sheer awfulness when the idea of *The Cool Boffin* first popped into my head.'

Pete Johnson has been a film extra, a film critic for Radio 1, an English teacher and a journalist. However, his dream was always to be a writer. At the age of ten he wrote a fan letter to Dodie Smith, author of *The Hundred and One Dalmatians*, and together they communicated for many years. Dodie Smith was the first person to encourage him to be a writer.

He has written many books for children as well as plays for the theatre and Radio 4, and is a popular visitor to schools and libraries.

Some other books by Pete Johnson

FAKING IT
I'D RATHER BE FAMOUS
TEN HOURS TO LIVE
MIND READER DOUBLE
THE PROTECTORS

For younger readers

BUG BROTHER
PIRATE BROTHER

THE
COOL BOFFIN
PETE JOHNSON

PUFFIN BOOKS

PUFFIN BOOKS

Published by the Penguin Group
Penguin Books Ltd, 80 Strand, London WC2R 0RL, England
Penguin Putnam Inc., 375 Hudson Street, New York, New York 10014, USA
Penguin Books Australia Ltd, 250 Camberwell Road, Camberwell, Victoria 3124, Australia
Penguin Books Canada Ltd, 10 Alcorn Avenue, Toronto, Ontario, Canada M4V 3B2
Penguin Books India (P) Ltd, 11 Community Centre, Panchsheel Park, New Delhi – 110 017, India
Penguin Books (NZ) Ltd, Cnr Rosedale and Airborne Roads, Albany, Auckland, New Zealand
Penguin Books (South Africa) (Pty) Ltd, 24 Sturdee Avenue, Rosebank 2196, South Africa

Penguin Books Ltd, Registered Offices: 80 Strand, London WC2R 0RL, England

www.penguin.com

First published 2003
2

Set in 11.5/15.5 Linotype Goudy
Typeset by Rowland Phototypesetting Ltd, Bury St Edmunds, Suffolk
Made and printed in England by Clays Ltd, St Ives plc

British Library Cataloguing in Publication Data
A CIP catalogue record for this book is available from the British Library

ISBN 0–141–31545–8

The Cool Boffin *is dedicated to the
cool team at the 'Big Toe Show' (R7)*

and

*to my effortlessly cool editor,
Yvonne Hooker.*

'And the sunlight clasps the earth,
And the moonbeams kiss the sea –
What are all these kissings worth,
If thou kiss not me?'

'Love's Philosophy',
Percy Bysshe Shelley

Contents

Boffin

This is my own true story of what happened when two months ago I decided to be someone different.

I'd better explain something first: for the first fifteen years of my life I was one of the nonentities: a boffin.

A boffin, of course, is an incurable swot, someone who gets such a high by being a good boy and doing all his homework that he can't stop – ever. So he swots and swots while the world passes by in a blur.

That was me. Perhaps I scuttled past you one day, thick glasses complete with sticking plaster, shirt collar down to my knees and my speciality: a knitted jumper, the sort where the neck hangs down and the cuffs are mega-wide.

Recognise me now? Don't worry if you don't. I'm sort of instantly forgettable. Day in, year out I'd dream of escaping my boffin image. But I never did anything. No bottle, I suppose.

And then, one day something happened – something

weird – and scary, I'd really like to tell you about it. So why not follow me over the page, where it's early morning and the first crazy event is just starting . . .

First-time Skiver

I'd been wanting to do it for fifteen years. And today, I finally did it. At 7.49 a.m. to be precise.

There I was, on the first day of term, which is always colder, darker and more depressing than any other day, waiting with all the wrinklies for that especially early bus which I'd never missed – until today. For today the bus pulls up, the queue slowly and stiffly get aboard and I don't move. I can't. My mind's screaming, 'Move' but my body won't obey. It's like those dreams when your body suddenly seizes up and try as you might you can't get it going again.

It's so weird and frightening. I can only compare it to when you sit on a nerve and find your foot's gone to sleep and is temporarily unmovable. Only this time, it's as if my entire body's gone to sleep. Of course, all the wrinklies are giving each other discreet nudges and squinting away at me frozen to the spot, until the bus finally wheezes off and then it's as if my power supply is switched on again.

For a moment I shuffle around unsteadily, holding on to the bus-stop – and looking like someone who's taking their first, faltering steps on the ice. But then my legs start feeling a part of me again. So what happened? And what do I do now? I could wait for the next bus and still get to school in plenty of time. I could do that. But I don't. Instead, I stumble away from the bus-stop and towards the common.

I'm skiving off. No-one's more amazed than me. I've never missed a lesson – or a homework, come to that – in my life. But here I am ... I must be in some kind of trance. Or perhaps I've been hypnotised without me even realising it.

But by the time I reach the common I wonder if it's everyone else who's been hypnotised. For there's neither a sight nor sound of human life. Just this strange, hushed deathly silence as if something's about to happen. Something bad.

I peer around me, feeling oddly defenceless, like an animal caught in the open. It's actually a relief to hear the thin screech of a train; somewhere, people know where they are going.

That sound reassures me. I'm being silly. The common's bound to be silent; after all, everyone's at work. Except me. I'm skiving off – and that's supposed to be enjoyable. So I'd better start enjoying it.

After checking for dog dirt, I plonk myself down. If

Mum could see me now she'd have a blue fit. Not so much at me skiving but at me sitting on grass which could be damp. I sit there, dazed and confused, thinking of nothing in particular. I can do that for hours. Then I peer at my watch. Nine o'clock. I am now an official skiver. At this very moment, Ma Divvy will be opening the register, and saying, 'Come on, quieten down while I take the register. This is a legal document, you know.' I hate it when she says that, also the way she's always saying 'That would be terrif . . .' but apart from that she's a good teacher. And when I don't answer my name she'll say with an edge of concern in her voice, 'Has anyone seen Richard Hodgson today?' And then the jokes will come pouring out. All those millions of jokes about me.

You see, I'm not a pretty sight. From a distance I'm easily mistaken for a basketball, up close I look all geeky and innocent . . . like someone Walt Disney forgot to draw.

Then last summer my form went swimming. I'd learnt to swim ages ago so I thought I'll dive into the pool and impress everyone with my aquatic skill. That's what I thought. Instead . . .

Have you ever belly-flopped your way into a swimming pool and seen your trunks pass before your eyes? Well, I have, but I really wouldn't recommend it. What's more, as I demonstrated the belly-flop, I caused a gigantic tidal wave which drenched everyone within a five-mile radius. It was the talk of the school for weeks. I even had requests for a repeat performance.

Then someone drew a picture of me belly-flopping on to dry land and looking like some great beached whale – underneath he inscribed the words 'SAVE THE BOFFIN'. This started a craze. Wherever you looked there were cartoons of great blubbery, bespectacled whales who were either reading a book or looking like a nerd – or both. And underneath, the phrase that haunts me – and probably always will – 'SAVE THE BOFFIN'.

Often I'd find Boffin creations thoughtfully pinned on to my locker. The artists would usually be hiding in the corner, anxious to catch me looking in their mirror. 'Recognise yourself, Boffin?' they'd say. I'd nod glumly. But otherwise, I wouldn't react. Inside, though, I'd be so mad and bitter. I know someone has to be lumbered with the short, fat, ugly body. But why me? I can't think of a part of me I wouldn't trade in for a newer, slimmer, hunkier model.

For now I'm stuck with this duff equipment. My one consolation is it's only temporary. I'm just going through a phase. At the moment, I've got these excitable hormones which are messing me up. Especially my face – which is exploding with zits so big they need to be detonated, not burst. But they'll calm down. I'm going through a phase. It's just a shame that this boffin carcase prevents people from seeing the real me.

The real me. I can't see the real me in this bright, cruel light. I close my eyes. There I am. I can see myself really clearly when my eyes are shut. I think you'd like me – a good bloke, you'd say. Even got a cool name: Ricky. Ricky is tall and slimmer than me, a top man actually – and looks more than a bit like Steve Almond. About now, Steve Almond'll stroll into school: ear-ring, trainers, no trace of school uniform and a massive grin blooming all over his face as he says in his sarky polite voice, 'So sorry I'm late.' Gets away with it every time.

You see, he's tall, cool, got a lot of bottle and girls fancy him like crazy. Even Anna Davies, who's probably the most good-looking girl in the universe. Of course at night I'd imagine Anna with Ricky. Some nights I have to switch the lights back on she gets Ricky so excited. I imagine her now as I dream on – and on. I wake up with a start. Anna Davies is sniffing my private parts. No, it's not Anna Davies, it's an Alsatian.

'Roma' the dog reluctantly leaves me and bounds towards the owner of that commanding voice. A big, tough-looking woman, who appears to be wearing about seven jerseys, strides past, swinging a stick and giving me a really funny look.

'Everything in order?' she asks.

'Yes, fine,' I say airily as if I normally spend my mornings sleeping on the common. And suddenly I realise I know her. Or my mother does. She's been round our house. I know she has. My heart starts trampolining. I wait for her 'Aren't you Mrs Hodgson's lad?' What can I say, 'No, I'm his naughty twin brother'? But instead, she just snaps 'Best to keep moving this weather,' and stomps away. She didn't recognise me. But she must do, she's been round our house enough. Just shows the impact I have on people – once seen, hastily forgotten. Unless – unless she's going straight round to see Mum. If that happens Mum'll go up the wall and stay there.

By twelve o'clock the skive is over and I'm back on the bus. I'm going to say I didn't feel well and went off to the woods to throw up. I went to the woods because I didn't want to mess up the pavement. Will they believe that? Of course they will. One of the very few perks of being a boffin is that adults always believe you.

I sit on the bus, locked away in my own bewildered thoughts. I couldn't tell you who else is on the bus or what they're staring at.

I arrive at the torture factory for the end of lunch. A damp mist still looms over the school, making everything look so blurred and out of focus I actually cheer up. I skulk past the lads on the back field. I can hear them shouting and laughing. Normally Tim Grant – a guy who enjoys giving me a hard time – would be hurling insults at me. But not today, I'm hidden by a layer of protective weather. And ahead lies every boffin's sanctuary: the library.

I check my runway carefully. All clear except – except for Anna Davies. She's walking past the library, past me and towards the back field. I treat myself to one loving glance. How does she always manage to look even better in real life than in my dreams? I go on treating myself. Why not? It doesn't matter to Anna. She won't even notice. I wait for her to slip past. As usual.

But instead she stops in front of me, eyelids quivering

and looking at me so strangely, you'd think she'd never seen me before. I gape back at her in amazement, imagining crazy things like I've woken up on the common in someone else's body. How else can I explain what happens next? For Anna makes as if to touch my shoulder, falters, and then sways forward into my arms.

Zombies Can't Die

For the first time ever, a girl lay in my arms. To get there, she had to be unconscious though. So in true boffin fashion I just held Anna limply and whispered, 'Are you all right?' I blushed as I said it but I couldn't think what else to say – then.

She tried to speak.

'Sorry,' I said. When in doubt, say 'sorry', a boffin motto.

'Chair, get me a chair,' she gasped.

'A chair!' I cried to the crowd which was gathering around us.

A little kid darted into the library. Two seconds later he darted out again carrying a chair, closely followed by the guy who'd been sitting in the chair. I flung Anna down. Her head flopped forward. Then I whispered, 'Would you like some water?'

At this her eyes suddenly sprang open and she gave me

that weird 'Who are you?' look again. My crazy idea came back. I've woken up in someone else's body. That'd be so great.

But then Anna lifted her head up and guided her hands towards my face. Next she ran very long, very red nails up and down my chin. I was quite happy for her to do this as long as she wanted but instead she said – and I'll never forget this, never – 'You're not a ghost, are you?'

'No,' I replied. 'I don't believe so.'

She started laughing and half shouted, 'I thought I was having a vision, like in that film when a dead person steps out of the mist.' She added casually, 'I really thought you were a ghost, you know.'

I shivered suddenly and felt a tightness at the back of my throat. No, I mustn't panic, must stay calm, keep a clear head so I can make sense of this.

'Hey, Boffin – what's the deal?'

It was Danny, a West Indian guy built like a tank, pushing his way through to me. 'We thought that you . . .' he faltered while I started shivering again. It was difficult to stop now, for I'd sensed something, something bad.

Danny turned to Anna. 'So what gives? Make with the info.'

'Don't ask me. I was walking over to see you and Steve just after Ash had told me about –' she lowered her voice '– about Boffin, when out of nowhere there he was, just standing there in the mist. It was so weird – like a haunting or something – and I fainted.'

'Did you really?' said Danny. He sounded quite

impressed. 'Can't imagine you fainting. Okay now?'

'Just about,' said Anna.

Danny whirled round to me. 'You got any injuries?'

'No.'

'No cuts or bruises?'

I shook my head.

'But you were there?'

I looked up at him. Where did he think I'd been? I was about to reply, to say I didn't know what he was talking about when I seemed to black out for a moment. All I could see was darkness and something, yes, there was something out there in the dark. And then it was as if a flash bulb had exploded in my head, for I could see the something really clearly. Only it wasn't a something. It was a body sprawled over a seat, splattered with blood.

A sharp terror seized me. 'It's horrible,' I gasped.

'What? What did you say?' Danny drew nearer, then called out, 'Steve, get over here.'

I started blinking furiously as if trying to rub away what I'd just seen. And I deliberately focused my gaze on the now sizeable crowd who were gawping at me as if I were on a stage. At the back I spotted Mouse, a fellow boffin from my form. If only I could get to him, perhaps he could explain all this. But he kept getting pushed further and further away from me – unlike Steve.

Steve didn't push and shove his way through to me, the crowd parted automatically for him.

Steve was one lad who never hassled the boffins and he patted me on the back in quite a friendly way. My eyes drew level with his school tie. He had cut off most of it, just the stub remained. I couldn't help admiring his nerve – and style.

'We heard about you this morning,' he said. 'Nasty. But you're all right?'

'Yes,' I croaked.

I took in a glare from Steve's shadow, Tim Grant. Trust him to be there. Steve turned to Anna. 'And why are you sitting down? Old age?'

'I fainted,' said Anna.

I watched her smile at Steve, saw him smile back – smiles that were more than smiles. She stood up beside Steve.

'But I'm fine now – you sit down there, Boffin – and tell us exactly what happened.'

As I fell into her place the image of that twisted body ripped through my mind again. Why did I keep seeing that? Where had it come from?

'Let me through, please, please, I'm collecting money.'

Ashley Saltmarsh, a girl from my form, was pushing her way through the crowd, waving four of the world's drabbest paper bags and breathlessly declaring, 'I thought I'd save giving out my party invites until tomorrow as a mark of respect. Already tried our form room but nobody had any money on them. So come on, you lot, cough up, I want at least 10p each.'

'Ash,' said Anna warningly.

She looked across and down before sighting me and gaping, 'Boffin! But I've just been out . . . er . . .' At once

13

she flung the collection bags behind her back as if they were her underwear.

Steve laughed, and flung the bags into the crowd as if he were throwing them out to sea.

Ashley knelt down in front of me. 'This is the most embarrassing moment in my life.'

I tried to smile at her but my face felt as if it was in the deep freeze.

'You still look very dazed,' she said.

'He always looks like that,' snapped Tim Grant.

'Oh, don't be wicked,' said Ashley.

I think she must have felt really sorry for me for she started smoothing my forehead.

'But you're freezing cold!' she exclaimed. 'Let's feel your hands – they're freezing too,' and she began to gently rub them.

I think my hands were beyond warming up, but it was extremely nice of her to try.

I was wondering idly who Steve was going out with – Ashley or Anna – when I heard Tim Grant sneer, 'Ash'll have a job warming up Boffin. Still, I've just worked out how Boffin escaped. Zombies can't die, can they?'

There was some scattered laughing while I tried to beam a look of pure hatred Tim Grant's way. But Ashley was already on her feet. 'Don't be so mean, Grantie. He's still in a state of shock and if the bus you'd been on had crashed this morning down Crendon Street, wouldn't you be dazed and shocked too?'

The skin on my face started pulling tighter and tighter

as if I was wearing a mask that was too small for me, while my mouth had this awful sick taste in it, especially when I thought of my bus crashing. That's what I'd seen in my blackout. I'd somehow seen one of the injured. And I could have been among them, caught up in an accident before the rest of my form were even awake. A victim of my boffin habits.

Danny was spieling on now, 'I heard about the Boff's accident first, 'cause I was in Matron's room when the Boff's old dear rings up. Got a loud voice, your mum, hasn't she?'

'My mum.' I immediately slumped down in my chair. I knew she'd be in this somewhere. Danny went on but his voice sounded oddly hollow and distant.

Your old dear starts gabbing about this really mean bus crash and it was the 7.49 which crashed, the Boff's bus, and he's not listed among the injured, but there's one body that's unidentifiable.'

At that point Danny's voice started to cut out and I felt myself being pulled towards . . . no, I don't want to go back there. To my relief, I hear Danny again.

'Well, old Matron's convinced the Boff is at school and I hear her telling the Boff's mum that he's safe and well. After Matron put the phone down I tell her I don't think the Boffin is at school. If you'd seen her face then . . . So there's this big search party for the register only no-one can find it. Everyone's going ape by now. It was great.' Danny smacked his lips appreciatively.

'Anyway, finally it turns up in Ma Divvy's desk. She'd forgotten to send it over to the office, Boffin normally takes it. So then when they found out the Boff wasn't marked in, they started getting out the old prayer mats. And although none of them would admit it, I knew they reckoned Boff was the unidentified body, cos he always sits in the front seat – well, he does at school and everywhere else, I bet. And the front seats are where people get it worst. So come on, Boff, tell us how you escaped.'

I could sense everyone moving in, enclosing me. And no-one was talking any more, instead there was this heavy, eerie silence just as there'd been on the common a few hours earlier. And if I hadn't skived off and gone to the common . . . the darkness curled over me, beckoning me . . . it was as if I was going into a trance, another state . . . perhaps that's why my voice sounded so muffled.

'My bus was coming down the hill when someone darted across the road. I heard the driver swear, as he jammed on his brakes and swerved. All at once the bus started shooting about, swinging around. And then, the bus suddenly lurched forward and ploughed through a building. Bricks started hitting windows and –'

'What building was it?' asked Steve.

'A hairdresser's,' I replied without even thinking.

'Can you imagine having your head in the sink and suddenly there's this bus up your backside?' interrupted Tim Grant.

'Oh, that's sick,' said Anna. She leant forward confidingly. 'Was there much blood?'

As she spoke I saw again that same twisted body. Only this time I see two ambulance men placing my body on a stretcher. The body is streaked with blood. One guy is putting a blanket on the body. Wait a minute, that body, it isn't me. Is it? It couldn't be. And is he going to cover that body, my body with a blanket? If he does that, it means . . . Suddenly I feel very weak, totally drained of life, and it's as if I'm being pulled into that body under the blanket but if I do that I'll never be able to come back, I'll be lost out there . . . I jump to my feet, choking with fear.

'Look at him, poor thing,' cried Ashley.

'Sick . . .' I said. 'I'm going to be sick.'

At once Steve took my arm. I gripped him hard.

'It's all right,' he said. 'You be sick, if you want. Follow me.'

The crowd started to follow. 'Get lost, you peg-legs!' said Steve, 'being sick is a private business.'

I could hear the crowd buzzing with disappointment. They wanted more blood and gore.

'Shall we get Matron?' asked Ashley.

'Nah, she'll only give him an aspirin. Get Ma Divvy if you like though.' Then to me, 'Now, go as slowly as you want.' Only Danny accompanied Steve and myself outside.

'How about puking up outside old Fungus Face's room?' said Danny.

I was keen to oblige. But although I felt all clogged up, nothing actually fell out. It was as if the sick feeling had gone too deep to be removed that easily. And I staggered back to Steve and Danny, feeling more gutted than ever. They'd been joined by Anna, Ashley and Ma Divvy.

'Don't you think Bof– Richard should go home?' Ashley said to her.

'Yes, I do. Richard, I'm so glad you're safe,' cried Ma Divvy, shaking me by the hand. She seemed genuinely chuffed. But then she said, 'Shall we just pop in and see the Head?'

When teachers refer to 'The Head' I always imagine this gigantic, disembodied head bobbing about. Not that I'd ever set eyes on 'The Head' up close. Was I about to?

'I know he'll be relieved Richard is safe and well,' said Ma Divvy.

'Bet he doesn't even know who he is,' murmured Steve.

Ma Divvy put her arm on my shoulder. 'We'll quickly go and see the Head while you all go to registration.'

'What's the point of that?' said Steve. 'You won't be there. We may as well have a few more minutes' break.'

'Steve, go to registration, please,' cried Ma Divvy as she half-guided, half-pulled me towards the main block.

'Don't take any hassle from Slap-Head,' called Steve. 'Any trouble and we'll sort him out for you.'

I turned round to see Steve and Danny speeding off in the opposite direction to the form-room. I waited, sentry-like, outside the Head's – or, to give him his proper title, Slap-Head's office. Normally only bad boys stood here. And I had been a bad boy, only no-one would ever guess that. Then I heard his door creak open and Ma Divvy say, 'Yes, yes, thank you very much, Headmaster,' as she walked out backwards. I don't think she curtseyed. 'The Head is delighted you are safe,' she gushed. 'He's asked me to tell you that he prayed for you.'

'Does he want to see me?' I asked.

'Well, not right now,' began Ma Divvy. 'He's rather busy at the moment . . .'

So even my rising from the dead wasn't enough to grant me a moment of Slap-Head's time. I think Ma Divvy sensed my anger – and hurt – for she tried to change the subject. 'I expect your mother's relieved.'

And that awful sick feeling came back, stronger than ever. My mother.

'She does know?'

I shook my head.

'Oh Richard, your poor mother,' said Ma Divvy. 'Matron has just told your mother you weren't at school and your mother was understandably very distressed. So we must ring her again right away.'

Two minutes later torrents of words burst through the receiver. Ma Divvy's head shook as the words poured into her. I took the receiver and managed to say, 'Hello, Mum,' before it was unleashed again.

This was nothing to the performance when I arrived home today. My mother can make a drama out of being interrupted on her hoovering day, so when a real crisis happens along she blows a fuse. Luckily, she spent the first couple of hours answering phone calls from neighbours anxious to hear of my fate. She'd alerted half of Wycombe, I think. But that was her way. Then, to my surprise, she put the phone off the hook and said, 'No more calls for a while. I want you to tell me, Nip, exactly what happened.'

I looked at her intent face. She wasn't seeking a cheap sensation, she really wanted to know, to experience what I'd experienced. I was tempted to tell her the truth. Be a good boy. Own up. Mum, I have skived and in doing so saved my life. But I didn't. Instead I went back out there and described it all. Once again horror seemed to fill me, leaving my throat so clogged up it was difficult to breathe afterwards. After I finished, Mum let out a small sob.

'I'll go and make us a nice pot of tea,' she said, but I knew she was really going away to have a few more sobs while I just sat there, amazed at me, a boffin, being able to tell such a total pack of lies.

A few minutes later I was in the kitchen. It was five o'clock. I was getting my tray ready as usual, Mum had the radio on as usual. And the smooth, bland tones of the guy who reads the local news were just one of many background noises . . . for a few moments the kettle coming to the boil threatened to annihilate him completely. Then, just as the kettle clicked itself off, Mum gasped, 'Listen – it's on the news!'

'. . . *the bus swerved to avoid a pedestrian, skidded on treacherous black ice and, while temporarily out of control, collided into Steven's hairdressing salon in Crendon Street. Fortunately there was no-one in Steven's salon at the time of the accident. But several of the bus passengers were taken to hospital suffering from shock. Mr Edward Albert, who was seated in the front seat, was knocked unconscious by the force of the crash. He suffered from a fractured jaw and temporary loss of memory but his condition was described as comfortable by . . .'*

I stared increduously at our tiny radio. Somehow it had managed to broadcast my own private nightmare. Or rather, somehow I'd been able to tune into an event which had really happened. No wonder the bus crash seemed so vivid. I was picking up the details of a real accident, the one which had nearly involved me.

That night I was actually afraid to close my eyes. It seemed as if the bus crash was just waiting behind my eyes to re-play itself. Soon, though, new thoughts started to take over. I remembered reading about this TV actress who sensed something terrible before boarding a plane. She immediately cancelled her booking. That plane crashed seconds after take-off, when it lost an engine and quickly turned into a horrific fireball. Everybody on board was killed. The article said the actress had detected ripples from an event yet to happen.

I shivered. My premonition – if that's what it was – hadn't been as dramatic as that. No-one had been killed in my bus crash. I suppose it was quite a minor accident really. Yet, if I'd caught my bus I'd have sat on the front seat – where else do boffins sit? – and probably suffered the same injuries as what was his name? Edward Albert? Poor guy. Another thought struck me. Was it his injured body I'd seen? He'd be in hospital for a few more days at least.

Perhaps weeks. And that could have been me. Yet, by the sheerest fluke I've escaped my fate. Or was it a fluke? Was there some reason why I've escaped?

Is something important about to happen to me? Now that's a laugh, nothing ever happens to me. I'm a boffin . . . a zombie. That's what Tim Grant called me today. Cruel – but true. One of the walking, talking dead, that's me. That *was* me.

'Glass of water, dear, in case your throat gets dry.' Mum looms over me.

'Thanks, Mum.'

'Your dad'll be home soon but don't wait up. You still look a bit peaky.'

After she's left I switch off the light. And the dark isn't threatening any more. No, it is just a great, heavy curtain hiding my future. I peer through the darkness, beyond the darkness and see . . .

It's me. And will you look at me? New clothes, very smart haircut, definitely a cool guy. And look at me here: I'm only getting down at a party. Ashley's party this Friday. I'm actually quite a good mover, I think. Certainly everyone's looking amazed and impressed.

'But you can't be the Boff,' they cry.

I smile – a smile even cuter and cooler than one of Steve's.

'This is the real me,' I say. I can't say any more, crushed by all these girls piling around me. I try and say, 'Steady – one at a time, girls,' but instead I just start laughing with joy . . .

I can see it all so clearly. More clearly than ever before. Before I was just dreaming. I know that. But this time it all looks so real.

Because it *is* real.

For today the boffin body-snatcher caught a bus and disappeared forever, leaving the way clear for . . . A strange happiness invades me. What I see is really happening. I'm going to make it happen – at Ashley's party this Friday – that's where, for the first time, everyone's going to see the real me.

Boffin Elimination: Countdown

Three days to go: TUESDAY

Ashley was really nice about me going to her party on Friday. I mean, I'd dreaded asking her – I hate doing things like that – and I think she was pretty surprised, well, stunned actually, but she tried to pretend she'd planned to ask me anyhow. I knew she was lying but it was good of her to bother to lie. Anyhow, I got my invite without any hassle.

Next job was to get some money for new clothes. This proved harder.

My dad makes a joke (sort of) that after work on Tuesdays he throws his bag into the house first. If the bag isn't thrown back, he comes in. You see, Tuesday is Mum's ironing day and ironing puts her into this snappy, really quite nasty mood. So I hadn't intended asking Mum for the money that evening. Especially after the way she assaulted me when I arrived home.

'Did you take it easy today?' she demanded.

'Yes, Mum.'

'Hmm, you don't look like you've got your sea-legs back.'

'I haven't been ill, Mum.'

'You had a nasty shock and you're still very pale. No headaches?'

'No, Mum.'

'Pains anywhere?'

'No, Mum.'

'Well, you come and sit down, have a nice cup of tea.'

I began to sit down.

'After you've washed your hands.'

I stood up again.

'Wash them well, love, you've got all the dirt of the day on them and I'm forever wiping away your finger-prints.'

Mum's flow was interrupted by the phone.

'Now who can that be?'

Mum hardly ever got any phone calls. It was a quick call, whoever it was, for by the time I finished the hand-washing ritual, Mum was back in the kitchen. And amazingly, she didn't check my hands to see I had rubbed up the right degree of lather on them. Instead she said, 'You don't mind having your dinner early, do you, dear? Only, I've got to go out, going to see your sister.'

She said it a little too lightly.

*

My sister married and left home to live in Stevenage last year. She was currently highly pregnant.

'She's not having the baby?' I asked.

'No, no, not yet,' said Mum, but she seemed strung up. And even though I'd long since ceased to think of Kay as my sister, I still felt a sharp stab of worry.

'Kay is all right?' I hardly dared say it.

'Oh yes, yes. Just wants to see her old mum, that's all.'

But I knew that wasn't all.

'So you're going all the way to Stevenage tonight?' I said.

'Won't take long. I'll go as soon as your father gets in. Get your tray ready, will you?'

'It's ready.'

'Oh yes, of course it is.'

I'd never seen Mum so distracted. Surely this would be a good moment to ask, very casually, 'All right if I take a little bit of my savings out, Mum?'

'What for?' she demanded, suddenly alert.

I found myself wilting. 'Er, just thought I'd get some new clothes. I do need some.'

Mum gave me a quick, appraising look. 'Yes, you do,' then added, 'but there's no need to touch your savings. We'll go down the town one evening after school. What would you need? New trousers, new shirt and some new shoes, ones that don't let the wet in this time. How's that?'

How could I tell her that I wanted to – had to – pick my clothes alone?

'I don't want to put you to any trouble, Mum.'

She patted me absently on the head.

'You're a good lad. However, I don't want you touching your savings. That's your little nest-egg. So one day soon we'll go round the shops . . . you need socks too. Can't have enough socks.'

Dad arrived shortly afterwards. While I downed the mince (Mum's speciality) they whispered upstairs. I heard Mum say, 'And the Nip's all right.'

That's what they call me – the Nip.

Think that's nearly as bad as the Boffin.

But after they'd driven off to see my sister, the Nip did something which would have shocked his parents rigid: he rooted around in the bureau until he'd retrieved his savings book. You can't call it stealing. How can you steal something which belongs to you? With luck though, my parents won't discover what I've done for ages. While, I can now get myself all kitted out for Friday.

Two days to go: WEDNESDAY

Took ages to get to sleep. Then I had one of my night-mares about the bus crash. Really sicko one too. I was trapped under this pile of rubble and as I tried to pull myself out I banged my hand on a shoe. A shoe with a foot in it. My foot! Can see it now, all blood-stained and knobbly and definitely mine.

At school, some people I'd told about the accident came back, just in case I remembered any fresh bits of gore about my bus crash. But I wanted to forget the bus crash now, forever.

At lunchtime I collected a hundred pounds of my savings. I had to ask the woman twice where I had to sign, (she mumbled), but otherwise I thought I was pretty cool about it all. And it felt good having a hundred pounds in my pocket. I made for the shop where all the cool gang go, only it was already crammed full of kids from our school. They were even eating their sandwiches in there. So instead I made for this posher shop, a bit out of the town centre. Dead pricey in there too and overflowing with assistants.

About four surrounded me as I crept in.

'Can I help you?' they chorused.

'No, no, just looking, thanks.'

Very self consciously, I tried examining some jeans. I didn't know where to start. My fingernail skimmed over some blue cords.

'What size, sir?'

I whirled round. One of the assistants was baring his teeth at me. He repeated – 'What size, sir?' His manner was really creepy, yet the way in which he said 'Sir' sounded dead sarky. He can only have been a couple of years older than me.

'I'm size . . . large, I think.'

'Yes, I think so, sir.'

A small smile escaped as he handed me a pair.

'Changing room in there,' he said, drawing a curtain.

'Oh right,' I said. I hadn't really intended trying them on but I didn't like to make a fuss.

'All comfortable then?' he asked when I'd plonked myself inside. 'Good,' and he drew the curtains again. I felt as if I'd been placed in a cage. The sooner I'm out of here the better.

As I was squashing myself into the cords I heard someone whisper, 'Excuse me, sir.' I jumped. I felt like the whisperer could see me. 'Yes?' I whispered back.

'If I may say, sir, those trousers Vince has selected for you are a bargain at just £23.99. You won't get them any cheaper anywhere else, will you, sir?'

'No, I won't.'

I thought it best to agree. It was more than a bit spooky talking to this disembodied voice and I sprang out of the changing room before I heard any other voices.

I know it's silly but I felt all hassled and confused as I nearly walked into my assistant.

He gushed all over me. 'Now don't you look smart. Come on, take a look at yourself.' He propelled me towards the mirror.

A posse of assistants followed.

I looked at myself for a millionth of a second but I couldn't concentrate, not with a chorus of 'What an excellent fit. That's you, sir, it really is.'

I turned round. 'I'll take them,' I muttered.

'What you need now is a smart shirt to go with them,' said Vince.

He was addressing the other assistants, who were already rummaging around for shirts my size.

I had to run back to school, I'd stayed so long in that shop. I hadn't meant to buy everything there – still, it is supposed to be a trendy shop. I'm never going there again though.

I stuffed Friday's gear into my locker. It's risky leaving anything in a school locker. Not half as risky as leaving it at home though. I mean, my mum'll have to know when I have my new haircut but I think that'll be enough for her.

I was still thinking about that when SPLAT – water started trickling down my hair and on to my collar. I grabbed a water balloon off my neck, they were really popular in our school, and heard Tim Grant's mad screech.

'How totally pathetic,' I shouted.

Tim Grant bobbed into view, followed by two fourth-year cronies.

'What did you say, Boffin?' He sounded disbelieving rather than annoyed.

'How totally pathetic,' I repeated in a much softer tone.

He squared up to me. (We're about the same size.)

'Don't hit him, Grantie, he's been in that bus crash,' called one of his cronies.

'I'm not going to hit him,' said Tim Grant. 'I just want an apology.' He was trying to sound easy and cool, like Steve does, but his voice shook.

'Come on, Boffin, apologise,' he demanded.

Normally I would have done. Normally I wouldn't have dared call him names. But what had he called me on Monday – a zombie?

Fired by that memory I found myself aiming the still partially full water balloon right into his face – then legging it like crazy. I could hear his friends cackling really loudly and Tim Grant muttering something and I knew he'd be out to get me. But for one moment I didn't care. I was too exhilarated by a rare and beautiful sight: one water balloon leaking all down Tim Grant's face.

One day to go: THURSDAY

Mouse and I usually meet up on the way to school. A sort of boffin alliance. Except Mouse doesn't look anything like me. He's got this really huge head and a long, painfully skinny body. I mean, when Mouse stands sideways he's a missing person. Crazy really. He can't gain weight; I can't get rid of it. We've been nicknamed the Brighton boys – me being the beach ball and Mouse the surfboard. And incidentally, Mouse has always been called Mouse – perhaps because his real name is Scott and he just doesn't look like a Scott.

Today, I sensed Mouse was in a picky mood, especially when he suddenly said, 'What's this about you going to Ashley Saltmarsh's party on Friday?'

'Yes, I'm going.'

'Why?'

'Why not?'

'But you never go to their parties.'

'Going to this one.'

He spluttered exasperatedly, just like my grandad does.

'But what is the point of going? It'll be just like the rest of their parties, consisting of a collection of people – most of whose IQs are scarcely any higher than their shoe sizes – all eating and drinking too much.'

'You're only jealous,' I teased.

'Jealous? I can assure you, Richard, I have better things to do with my time than attend such utterly puerile events.'

Mouse was getting really worked up. As usual, when he got excited globules of white liquid sprayed out of the side of his mouth. I challenged him further, perhaps because it was a bit like challenging myself.

'So what are you going to do on Friday night then? Sit at home poring over a few tasty textbooks? You'll never meet anyone at home, certainly no decent girls.'

'At the moment I'm too busy to meet girls.'

'At the moment,' I sneered.

'Yes, there'll be plenty of time after I have passed all my examinations. Then I shall be ready to meet young ladies and I'll have something to offer them, while all the rest of our class will be clambering around on the dole.'

'You reckon?'

'Certainly.'

He wiped his mouth and as usual, traces of white remained on his hand.

'When they're all burnt out I'll be entering my peak.'

He squinted through his glasses at me as if he was trying to get me into focus. 'All this party talk. It's probably the shock of the accident. You haven't recovered your equilibrium yet, but . . .'

A now familiar SPLAT and a water balloon landed at our feet. I heard someone shout 'Nearly!' then one of Tim Grant's gang leapt out of the bus shelter.

'You should have got 'em,' called out his mate. 'They were such an easy target.'

'Too easy,' he said, retrieving his prize possession. He dangled it in Mouse's face. Mouse froze.

'We thought your hair needed washing,' he taunted.

Mouse's shoulders were hunched but his face was a complete blank.

Then Tim Grant called across the road, 'The Boffin's going to Ashley's party!' He said it as if he was telling a joke.

'Can't wait to see the Boffin – head-banging,' he continued.

His mates laughed. And as we sidled past them, Tim Grant yelled out, 'I'll settle up with you tomorrow night, Boffin.'

When we were out of earshot, Mouse came alive again.

'If any of that lot have a brain operation it will cost 24p and that will include search fees.'

Mouse can be really funny about people behind their backs. But I knew he was talking big now because he'd been scared. And he was still breathing away like a suction pump, while he snarled, 'That's the sort of moron you're going to be mixing with on Friday. Do you really want to be like that?'

I whirled round to face Mouse and he rocked back as if a gust of wind had hit him. 'No, Mouse, I don't want to be like that but I don't want to be like us either, scurrying away as soon as anyone says "boo" to us, everyone laughing at us and pitying us – and pushing us around and . . .'

'But don't you realise this is just a phase?' said Mouse wearily.

'I know we say that, but is it? I mean, we could go on like this for years.'

'Rubbish, in a few years we'll be . . .'

'A few years – in a few years I'll be old. I can't wait a few years. Don't you realise that this is the time when we're supposed to be out doing things, experiencing things? It may already be too late. But if I don't try now I'll never catch up. Never.'

Mouse examined me as he might a particularly difficult algebraic equation. He stood there frowning hard, looking like an elderly six-year-old. Last week he'd been my closest ally, now I felt we were light years apart.

'If you go on Friday, you'll regret it,' he said suddenly.

'Why?'

'You just will,' he said.

'How do you know?'

He didn't answer, merely looked grave, like a doctor who doesn't relish breaking the results of his examination.

'You'd like me to fail, wouldn't you?' I cried.

'Well, if that's what you think, there's nothing more to be said,' said Mouse stiffly. 'Anyhow, I must go. I don't want to be late. Soon, I expect you will have to be late if you're to keep in with the morons you worship.'

He stalked off. But I sensed he was more hurt than angry. Like me. We sat apart all day.

I couldn't forgive him for saying, 'If you go on Friday you'll regret it.' Perhaps I will regret it. But he shouldn't have said it. Anyway, what have I got to lose? I'm already a boffin and you can't get any lower than that, can you?

The final countdown – FRIDAY

I slipped through the back door wearing a new hairstyle and feeling like I'd just pulled the cap on a grenade. Any second now there'd be an almighty explosion and the fallout – the fallout – would be pretty intense. But there wasn't the expected blow-out in the kitchen because Mum wasn't in the kitchen.

Her voice spewed in, though. 'Is that you, Nip?'

'No, it's a burglar,' – a tiny joke before the big bang.

'You're very late. Hurry up and wash your hands then you can help me with the new cabinet. Tried getting it upstairs but it's heavier than I thought. Use plenty of soap.'

I used gallons. Anything to ward off the dreaded

encounter of a close and furious kind. Then, in a kind of slow motion, I opened the kitchen door and glided towards the voice, which was sprawled over a cabinet at the bottom of the stairs.

'I've been all day assembling this. It's supposed to take half an hour. Still, what can you expect when the instructions are in Japanese? Right, show me your hands. I don't want your dirty fingerprints over my nice new cabinet, it's mahogany veneer.'

Her eyes made contact with my anatomy. First a careful perusal of the hands.

'You haven't washed all the soap off. Still, you're improving. Just remember to give them a good rub!'

Then her eyes quickly skimmed upwards. 'And when you . . .' A gasp of horror as she finally faced me. Then another larger gasp, after which my mum was speechless. She must have been very shocked.

And then, 'Your hair – what have you done to your hair?'

'Been to the hairdresser's, Mum.'

'But look at it! Look at it!' She was growing hysterical.

'Don't you like it?'

'No, it's far too short. Why, you're nearly bald!'

'That's the fashion, Mum.'

'The fashion? You look a disgrace. An absolute disgrace!'

'I like it,' I said quietly.

'It's awful. Quite awful. Makes you look like one of those punky hooligans.'

'Mum, it's just short. A quite normal style for these times.'

However, Mum was beyond reasoning.

'Oh, how could you do this to yourself?'

I tried to change the subject. 'Shall we take this cabinet upstairs?'

'As if I haven't got enough to contend with, what with your sister –' She stopped suddenly.

'What about my sister?'

'Oh, nothing – nothing compared to you. Look at you.'

I started pushing the cabinet upstairs by myself.

'No, no!' cried Mum. 'You'll strain yourself on your own.' She tried to push me aside and we both almost lost our grip.

'Steady, steady,' I said.

Mum didn't reply.

We hoisted the cabinet up in silence. I steered it into Mum's (and Dad's) bedroom.

'Where do you want it?'

'Just leave it there, thank you.'

Mum fired another disapproving stare at me. 'They saw you coming.'

'Who?'

'The people at the hairdresser's. They knew they had a right soft lump coming in. Anyway, your face is too large for that hairstyle. Makes you look quite ugly.'

'Mum!' I screamed, banging my fist down on the cabinet. 'I like this hairstyle. I like it. And what's more, I'm going to a party tonight.'

'What party?' she demanded at once.

'A party at the village hall given by one of my form.'

'Who?'

'Ashley Saltmarsh.'

Mum's tone became suspicious. 'Is that a boy or a girl?'

'A girl.'

'Ah – and I suppose she put you up to this.' She pointed to my hair.

'No, of course not.' I was getting annoyed again. 'Why do you have to make everything so awful?'

'Me? I'm the one who keeps this house going single-handed. I'm the one who's got to get your tea now. Come and lay the table for me.'

She scurried downstairs, muttering to herself. I followed behind. She'd made me feel angry and ashamed so, trying to patch things up, I said, 'You don't really mind me going out, do you, Mum? I won't be late.'

'Do what you like!' she snapped.

I hate it when she talks like that, so I banged the knives and forks down and sprinted back upstairs.

Suddenly Mum called out, 'Will you be home for breakfast?'

'Depends whether I get a better offer!' I replied, slamming the door.

Trust Mum to spoil everything. And I'd really enjoyed myself in the hairdresser's. It was very busy there and yet everyone was so friendly. Never seen so many pretty girls either. My 'stylist' reminded me a little of Anna. Her name was Judy and she was very nice. Even asked me if I wanted a cup of coffee. Then she asked if I liked it 'white', how many sugars, and afterwards, 'Did you enjoy your coffee?' She really cared.

As for my hair: I examined it in my alarmingly large mirror. It suited me. Definitely. I'm sure it did. I certainly looked hard – well, harder. Just the image I wanted.

I started again. Was I good-looking now? Not quite. But then I don't have the rest of my gear on. And I need the clothes to set the hairstyle off.

Currently, my new clothes are stored under a seat on the common. I know it's dodgy leaving them there, I mean, right now some tramp could be strutting about in them. But can you imagine the performance downstairs if I'd worn all my new gear in the house? I couldn't handle that. It's really less hassle to leg it down to the common and get changed in the loos by the recreation centre.

'Tea!' Mum called. Her tone was distinctly chilly. I wish she liked my hair – a little. But that's my boffin side, wanting to please Mummy all the time.

I ate in the kitchen while Mum sat in the lounge. I knew she was having a sulk so I didn't disturb her and after I finished I washed up my plates, shouted, 'Thanks for a delicious meal,' and crept back upstairs.

I put on a ghastly knitted jumper and some pre-World War I grey trousers. I knew I could quite safely deposit these on the common while I was partying. Not even a tramp could be that desperate.

'I'll be off now,' I said.

'Your father wants a word,' said Mum.

Dad had just dropped in; he would be going out again a few hours later. Being a school caretaker meant he worked shifts and always looked knackered. Right now he was sitting in the lounge, dozing over a cup of tea. But he opened his eyes for a full ten seconds when I appeared.

'Hair's a bit short, isn't it, Nip?'

'It's the fashion.'

'Be cold these winter nights.'

'It's the fashion,' I repeated.

'I don't think your mother likes it.'

'It's not her hair.'

He stirred his tea reflectively.

'Of course I've seen boys at my school with hair as short as yours. Shorter. That's the way they have it now. I don't think your mother understands that. Give her time.'

He was trying to be nice, trying to understand.

'All right, Dad, I will.'

'Your mother says you're off to a party tonight.'

'Yes, Dad.'

'Need a lift?'

I was touched by the offer.

'No, no, it's at the village hall just up the road.'

'Oh, at the village hall, eh?'

'Yes.'

'Well, that's not far. The village hall, eh?'

He closed his eyes then opened them again, his voice fading away. 'Be back by eleven, Nip. Have a good time.'

He closed his eyes again. I knew they'd be locked shut for a couple of hours now.

Mum was hovering by the door.

'You've forgotten this.' She flung a revolting brown scarf round my neck. 'Put it right round you. There's a cold east wind tonight. And have you got your inhaler – just in case?'

'Yes, Mum.'

I felt annoyed with her again. I haven't had one of my asthma attacks for ages.

She did up the top two buttons on my coat.

'And keep buttoned up. It's bitter outside. Bitter.'

'Yes, Mum.'

She made me feel as if I was leaving home for good – not one evening.

'Watch out for yourself, son,' she said. 'There's some funny people about.' I shuddered.

'But enjoy yourself.' She patted my hair, 'I dare say it'll grow again soon.'

I didn't stay to explain that my hair would always be that short. Instead I sped towards the common and a dream that was about to come true.

ASHLEY
INVITES YOU TO
THE GREATEST PARTY EVER

FRIDAY Jan 7th
EIGHT O'CLOCK TO LATE
AT
THE VILLAGE HALL
BE THERE OR
BE SORRY FOREVER!

S.W.A.W.T.
Sealed with a wet tongue.

Ashley Invites You

'Who let you in?' His face was wrinkled with contempt. But not even Tim Grant could spoil my party. You see, I felt good.

I'd felt good ever since I'd changed into my new clothes. Even though I'd had to get changed behind this tree (the loo was locked up) and my clothes were freezing (normally anything I wear is cooked in the airing cupboard for at least a week) and more than a little crumpled. I just knew that I looked pretty okay.

And although I got some funny looks at the party, they were caused by the novelty of seeing a boffin in trendy gear. Anyhow, some people were really keen on my new look. Like Ashley, who'd said, 'Oh, you little devil,' in a really friendly way when she saw me and Anna, who'd gone, 'Oh wow!' She'd said 'Wow!' very slowly and it sounded a bit sarky – but I don't think it was meant to be. I really don't.

So, by the time Tim Grant started scowling and sneering at me I'd been at the party for over an hour. Practically everyone else including Tim Grant had arrived very late. I mean, the invite said 'eight o'clock' but when I arrived on the dot of eight hardly anyone else was there. I thought that was rather an insult to Ashley.

I managed to wedge myself in between a group of girls – including Ashley and Anna – and heard them passing comments on each new arrival. I don't think Ashley liked any of the girls she'd invited. Then Danny & Co. arrived and they circled around the girls, showing off their new clothes or, in Danny's case, his new gold sovereign ring. He showed every single girl its hallmark.

However, when Tim Grant stomped over there were only jeers and exaggerated laughing. For, like me, he'd had his hair done, only he'd given himself something called the 'wet look' (or as Danny called it, 'the gel look'). It didn't suit him at all – just made his hair look all flat and greasy – and everyone was calling out things like, 'It was a good joke, Grantie, but you can take the wig off now!' and Tim Grant tried to smile as he squirmed in front of us.

I'll be honest, I really enjoyed this spectacle, drinking in Tim Grant's misery with such pleasure that I suddenly, spontaneously, laughed. That's when Tim Grant said, 'Who let you in?' in his low, menacing growl of a voice. For years I'd had to endure every insult he threw at me but tonight the atmosphere felt different and I dared to reply, 'Is your hair stuck on?'

His eyes widened with amazement while his voice became lower.

'Do you know what you look like?'

For a second I faltered. But only for a second. He couldn't intimidate me. I looked pretty okay tonight, I knew that. So I replied, quite chirpily, 'Just so long as I don't look like you.'

I got a few laughs and Danny said, 'Look at Boffin standing up for himself.' He said it quite admiringly. Of course, I didn't like being called Boffin but the times were changing. And you should have seen the shocked look on Tim Grant's face as his punchbag suddenly turned on him. Tim Grant couldn't reply to me, to any of them. So instead, he turned his back on us. He'd tucked his T-shirt in so you could see the label on his jeans.

But then he quickly turned around again for Anna suddenly screamed, 'Oh no, Ash, get me my coat. I'm going. I mean it!'

'What's happened?' asked Ash, all alarmed.

'I've just seen this bloke. This bloke who keeps ringing me up and pestering me, begging me to go out with him.'

'Has he got a white stick?' asked Danny. And some of the girls looked rather annoyed with Anna. I think they thought she was trying to draw attention to herself.

'Is this guy very ugly?' asked one girl hopefully.

'No, no, not at all,' said Anna. 'And he's a really nice bloke. It's just he keeps ringing me – rang me four times one morning. And last night he came round and I ran upstairs and told my mum to say I was out. Yet what does she do? Only invites him in for a cup of tea. I bet she told him I was coming here.'

'Don't worry,' said Danny, 'we'll protect you from this wolfman.' He sounded pretty sarky. 'Where is he then?'

'There he is,' said Anna, pointing to a guy who was waving animatedly at her.

Instantly Danny dropped his sarky tone.

'You see what he's wearing, Grantie? A baseball jacket with Memphis on,' said Danny.

'And he thinks he looks the business,' went on Tim Grant. 'Just look at the way he's strutting about.'

Actually, his walk was identical to that of Danny and Tim Grant. But they were both getting really worked up now.

'Comes in here,' hissed Danny, 'as if he own the place . . . I think he needs to show us a bit more respect.'

He stared round at the other boys and without another word I sensed an army forming. The girls sensed it too.

'Now, no trouble please,' said Ashley.

'He's quite a nice guy, really,' said Anna, defending him now.

'Danny, I'll really get it in the neck if anything happens, please.' Ashley was begging.

'Ash, we don't want trouble but any bloke who swaggers about in a party the way he does . . .' Danny smacked his fist against his arm, 'well, he's just asking for it and . . .'

He was interrupted by music blaring out ten times louder than it had before and a smooth male voice welcoming everyone to Ash's Friday night party.

'The DJ's started,' said Ashley gratefully.

'Come on, everyone, get dancing.'

Danny gave Ashley a kiss. 'Don't worry, Ash, it'll be okay,' then he added ominously, 'I don't know what Steve'll do when he sees him, though.'

'Is Steve arriving soon?' asked Anna.

'Said he'd turn up when the pubs closed. Come on, lads, let's grab a bit of action.' Danny led his troops on to the floor. But as he left, Tim Grant whispered to me, 'First we'll get Memphis – then I'll get you.'

'Oh yeah,' I said rather weakly. However, his new attack had taken me by surprise. He slammed his fist against his arm, just like Danny had. 'I'll hit you so hard you'll go flying into next year.'

I tried to smile but this time I couldn't When you're a twenty-four-carat coward any threat of physical violence gets the palpitations going. Still, the rest of the blokes would never let Tim Grant attack me, would they?

I tried to forget Tim Grant and concentrate on the party. I stood watching a group of girls dance around their handbags. It was really weird, they put these small bags in the centre – some also bunged their shoes there – and then they did this nothing kind of dance. I mean, occasionally they'd move their toes about one centimetre, otherwise they concentrated on whispering, giggling and watching the blokes.

Meanwhile, a group of blokes led by Danny were jumping in the air, pretending to headbang each other, rhythmically thumping the guy next to them and watching the girls. No-one invited me to join in the dance, in fact, no-one was actually talking to me. So I did a spot of party circuiting, walking around the hall, pretending to examine the food and every so often watching the dancers and grinning enthusiastically as if I was really part of the scene.

At ten o'clock Steve arrived (the pubs must have closed early) and the party stopped for a full ten seconds. Unlike Danny and the others, he didn't strut in – in fact he shuffled along to the drinks table, deliberately not catching anyone's eye.

He didn't need to.

Steve just dug his hands down very faded jeans and smiled his 'I'm here, I'm cool and that's enough' smile. Then he poured himself a drink and the crowds swarmed around him, chattering away.

I liked Steve and when he nodded in my direction I felt almost ridiculously proud. But seeing how the girls reacted to him gave me real pangs of jealousy. The girls didn't speak to Steve but I could sense them tensing up, becoming watchful, ready in case he approached them.

It was like that – in a diluted way – when any bloke shot in, except me. Some girls were quite nice to me but in the way you'd be nice to some adult who'd wandered by. Now, I hadn't arrived here expecting a wild orgy, didn't feel quite ready for that yet, to be honest. No, tonight I'd have been content if one girl had looked at me and fancied me, just the tiniest bit. I didn't expect any action – I just wanted to know if girls saw me as the same gender as Steve.

'You haven't got a drink,' Ashley was staring at me, 'that's strictly against the rules.'

She swayed slightly and half-fell against me.

'Are you all right?' I asked.

She leant against my shoulder. 'Oh yeah, just a bit of trouble standing up.'

'My granny has the same problem.'

She laughed. 'Does she? That makes me feel much better.' She ran her hands up and down my hair. Felt quite nice.

'It's so short. Really short. And your clothes . . .'

'Yes?'

'All new, aren't they?'

I nodded.

'And yet you're not chilling, are you? Admit it.' She took my hand. 'Well, I'll help you chill. Follow me. Do you like wine?'

'I think so.'

She swayed over to the table, poured half the contents of a bottle of white wine on to the tablecloth and the other into a pint glass.

'Hey, steady!' I cried.

'Steady nothing. You're at a party. My party. You'll do as you're told,' she said. 'Now, drink it, all of it.'

I took a swig – it was quite sweet but not bad.

'Charming little vinegar,' I said, 'or is it iron filings?'

'No, it's nail varnish remover. Drink some more.'

I gulped down plenty more under Ashley's watchful eye. She was watching me like my mum did when I had to take cough medicine. Ashley's got sparkly eyes and a smiley face. She's also really pretty looking. And I said to her, 'You look ace tonight, Ashley.'

'Oh, you wouldn't say that if you'd seen my spot. No, no, don't look for it. I've hidden it with my concealer stick but it's there. I know it's there. Get one before every party. And tonight when I go home, the spot will dry up and be all mangy and flaky and disgusting and not nice.'

'Oh, but that's only one spot. I've got tons. They're all on the left side of my face, that's why I'm facing you with my right. I'll tell you something else, my spots grow at night while I'm asleep.'

'Just like mine. Drink some more wine – that's good for spots.'

I drank some more then I suddenly realised something. 'Where's your drink, Ash?'

She whispered into my ear. It tickled. 'I'm pissed already but I've got a good reason for being pissed.'

'Your spot?'

She swayed and nearly fell over with laughter.

'No, not that, something even more serious, something . . .'

'Now then, Ash, stop chatting up Boffin.'

Anna had just joined us. 'Are you all right?' She took hold of Ash.

'Fine, fine.'

'I wanted to tell you something, Ash.'

Anna gave me a 'Scram, please' look. I was hurt but said, 'Shall I go?'

'No, no,' said Ash. 'Stay. Go on, Anna,' and I sensed that Ash already knew what Anna was going to say.

Anna was clearly embarrassed. 'It's just – just, Steve has asked me to go outside.'

Clearly, going 'outside' meant something, for Ash gave a start but then said, 'Well go outside with him if it's what you want.'

'Oh, Ash.'

Anna had her arm round her and was rocking her gently.

'I don't want to hurt you, on your party night too.'

Ash seemed to sober up a bit and unhooked Anna's arm.

'That's all right, Steve's chucked me. And if he wasn't going outside with you it would be someone else.'

Anna didn't reply. There was an embarrassed silence then – 'At least Martin is off my back,' said Anna. 'He's done four slow dances with Katie Adams.' She pointed to Memphis, who was wrapped around a pretty girl from our form.

'Katie Adams!' said Ashley bitterly. 'She's so prim she blushes if she eats a hot dog.'

Anna, obviously anxious to join up with Ash in something, said, 'And have you seen her hair? Looks like she's got a cactus growing on top of it.'

'And I hate her voice,' went on Anna. 'She always talks as if she's got her finger up her nose.'

Ash laughed out loud at that comment. While she was laughing Anna whispered, 'See you later then, Ash,' and disappeared towards Steve.

At once Ash stopped laughing. I felt sorry for her and said, 'You and Steve seemed to go so well together – not that I know much about . . .'

'Anna always gets what she wants, so I'm not surprised,' interrupted Ash. She added, 'I'll have to leave you now, I'm going to throw up.'

I waited for Ash to return. But she didn't come back and it was probably just as well. For I don't think even she could have prevented what happened next.

Exposing a Fake!

Shortly after Ashley, everything changed. The DJ said, 'Now it's time to slow it down a bit,' but instead, everyone was on the move, trekking around the hall, trekking outside, returning inside, then back out again . . . endlessly going nowhere.

And charging through all the other travellers was a gang of about twenty blokes led by Danny and Tim Grant. They didn't speak or smile or even nod at me. But then, I don't think they saw me. However, just to brush past them was to receive a charge of high-voltage aggro. I'd have hated to have been subjected to a full blast.

Yet, their most obvious target was so busy entwining himself around Katie he didn't even seem to notice them. Not even when Tim Grant barged up to Memphis yelling, 'You looking for trouble, mate?'

'Go away,' murmured Memphis and returned to Katie's neck.

She kept giving little contented sighs so I guessed she was enjoying herself. No boys from our year had shown her so much attention. I'd heard them in class say her brace limited progress – but Memphis advanced on to the mouth with apparent ease.

I watched, fascinated. I was especially impressed with the way they could adjourn to the dance floor without disentangling their lips. Although they were the only couple dancing, Tim Grant still managed to bump into them.

'Watch it, Memphis,' he said. Memphis didn't even reply this time.

And then Steve was suddenly in the doorway. He looked a bit sinister, scarey, even. Funny, I'd never thought of Steve as frightening before, rather, he'd always been my protector. But now there was something eerie about the way a crowd was gathering expectantly around him while he just stood there, completely motionless and with a smile playing around his lips.

Then Anna appeared beside Steve. I wasn't as jealous as I'd expected. It seemed natural, somehow. She belonged alongside a rock star or a prince or Steve. She whispered something to him, he whispered back, and then they both disappeared from view.

Moments later came silence. The music just died in the middle of a song. Katie and Memphis stopped dancing and looked around them. They saw how everyone else was edging around the doorway. They were all alone.

'What's going on?' cried Katie, her voice cracking.

Danny didn't answer but began moving towards them,

followed by Tim Grant. Then he said, in a low whisper. 'They want you outside, Memphis.'

'Who does?' he asked.

'Everyone in here.'

Danny pointed to the rest of the party, clustered round the doorway.

'You're ruining their party, Memphis,' said Danny.

'I am?' he cried. 'How?'

'By having such a bad attitude,' snarled Tim Grant. 'You came in here as if you owned the place. And now you start messing about with one of our girls.'

'I'm not one of your girls,' murmured Katie. Memphis just blinked at them in astonishment.

'Now, are you going to come outside like a man?' demanded Danny.

'Like a man?' echoed Katie scornfully. 'It really looks it. The whole party against one person.'

'Steve is waiting,' said Danny impatiently.

'Look, leave him alone!' cried Katie, sounding very scared now.

Tim Grant butted in, 'You stay out of this, Katie, it's you we're doing this for.'

'Rubbish. You're doing it because you love fighting. You boys make me sick.' She appealed to the crowd. 'Can't you stop this?'

Her cries only roused Memphis.

'Look, who is so jealous of me and Katie?' He turned to Tim Grant. 'Is it you? Well why don't you get a girl of your own?'

In a fury, Tim Grant lashed out, aiming his fist at Memphis's jaw (he couldn't reach any higher), but Memphis was too quick, nimbly fielding the blow and stabbing his fist right in Tim Grant's stomach.

Tim Grant fell faster than the speed of light. Danny knelt down. 'I'm all right,' spluttered Tim Grant. Danny tactfully turned away. But I didn't. I saw Tim Grant rolling feebly around on the ground – it was like watching a fly which had had its legs torn off. Only I'd have felt sorry for the fly.

I watched him, long after all other eyes had turned towards Steve, who strode towards Memphis and, without a word, lifted him off the floor. One hand held his neck, and while Memphis gasped and Katie screamed, Steve said in a voice so reasonable it sent chills down my spine – 'We're going for a walk. You see, we promised Ash we wouldn't mess the place up and we always keep our promises.'

The crowd surged outside. So did I. But then I quickly turned away. The fight was Steve versus Memphis, only it was no contest. And it was all so pointless, so ugly, so nasty. So why were they doing it? And why was no one stopping it? I caught sight of some of the girls. They looked pretty sick, especially those around Katie. However, some of the others – they were standing there watching it all – as if it was a fight on TV.

A few were murmuring about it not being a fair fight but they only said that when they were back by the village hall. I followed them and I was so lost in revulsion

I'd temporarily forgotten about Tim Grant.

He hadn't forgotten about me, though. For as I entered the hall he was squaring up to me, shaking slightly. It was the shaking and the fact that I'd seen him on his back only five minutes ago that gave me a glimmer of confidence.

'Feeling better?' I said over-brightly.

'I will be when you stop pushing your nose in. And I'm going to smash your nose down to a blackhead.'

'Are you?' I tried to keep my tone light.

He shook some more. I think he was in pain. I hoped so. Then he stood right in front of me, pressing down hard on my toe. I was relieved. If this was all he was going to do to me I could take it. No sweat. Perhaps he was too knackered to do anything else.

He removed his foot. 'That hurt?'

'No, it was really very nice,' I said.

Afterwards, I wished I hadn't tried to be funny for he whispered furiously, 'Well what about this?' and started whacking his fist across the side of my face. It was like being hit by an iron.

'All right, stop now. Please,' I begged.

He stopped. And as I staggered backwards on to the floor, my glasses sprang off my face and I started breathing in short spurts as if someone was strangling me. I also had this strange numbing ache in my cheekbone or where my cheekbone used to be. I'd just had it amputated. And I could hear the sea roaring away. How was that possible?

Someone touched my face. I flinched and blinked. The

world was coming a little more into focus. I was four-eyes again.

'You all right?'

'Who said that?' I tried to turn my head. Impossible. But then I heard, 'All right? He's never been all right!'

'Oh, leave him, he hasn't done you any harm,' said a mild voice.

'Yes he has!' cried Tim Grant, sounding a bit hysterical. 'Poking his nose into everything. And everyone, supposed to suck up to him because he's a poor, pathetic boffin. Well, I'm not going to. I tell the truth.' He paused. 'He comes poncing in here, thinking he's so great, trying to put me down – and look at him. Look at those clothes. Where do you hide on Guy Fawkes night, Boffin?' He gave his strange, high-pitched laugh.

To stop his laughing, I stuttered, 'You're only jealous.'

'Jealous! What of? Do you know what everyone's been saying about you?'

'No, Grantie, don't,' said that mild voice again.

'Why not? Why in hell not?' he exclaimed. 'We all have to take it, why shouldn't he? Anyway, he wants to know, don't you?'

Without waiting for my answer he raced on. 'My fat Boffin, everyone's been laughing themselves silly at you tonight. Only you're so weak and fragile and so enjoyed imagining you were cool that no one liked to tell you you've got it all wrong.'

I stumbled to my feet.

'You're not going, are you?' asked Tim Grant. 'Still, I suppose this is late for you.'

Suddenly, he started laughing again. He sounded like a dog yapping and the noise went right through my head.

But worse, far worse than anything he said were all these murmurs of sympathy beating down on me. They were pitying me!

Shapes circled around me, petting me, asking me if I was all right and generally behaving as though I was a lost puppy. I edged round them, grasped the door and nearly fainted as gallons of air burst over me.

But I was determined. I slunk past the crowd outside, wondering what had happened to Memphis. Nothing bad, I hoped. There was certainly a good deal of shouting. I thought I could hear Ashley. But deafening all the other sounds was that ghastly buzz of sympathy. Even though I'd left the hall far behind, I could hear them louder than ever, inside my head. I could even hear their thoughts, 'Poor Boffin. He tries. But he's got it all wrong again. Now don't laugh at him – you mustn't. Not within his ear-shot anyhow.'

How had I got it so wrong? Not even Tim Grant can hate me as much as I hate myself.

When I reached the seat in the woods I tore off my new clothes – clothes which I'd put on so reverently a few hours earlier. Now I didn't even bother to wrap them up in my PE kit-bag. Let the birds have them. I'll never wear them again.

Getting dressed was hard. My hands were so weak and shaky I couldn't seem to get a proper grip on either my trousers or shirt. I imagined some little old lady walking her dog, spying me and accusing me of flashing. She'd need a magnifying glass.

I finally stumbled home. The house was in darkness. I crept upstairs, not switching any lights on, even though I knew my mum wouldn't be asleep. And sure enough, as I crossed the landing:

'That you, son?'

'Yes, Mum.'

'Pulled the door tight?'

'Yes, Mum.'

'And bolted it?'

'Yes, Mum.'

'And did you have a nice time?'

'Yes, Mum. Very nice,' I replied.

If Brains Were Dynamite

Monday morning – a morning to rot my insides. For the whole school knew. If only all those girls hadn't smiled at me as if I was a war casualty who'd had all his vital parts blown off.

By lunchtime, like some wretched homing pigeon, I was back in the library among my boffin brothers, hunched over rows of books, carefully shielding ourselves from the ugly, messy world beyond.

I slipped into my usual place opposite Mouse. He was pouring himself into a large, dusty volume and coughing loudly as if he were swallowing it up too quickly. He ignored me.

'Mouse?'

His eyes darted over the barricade of books.

'I expect you heard what happened to me on Friday?'

He nodded solemnly. I half hoped Mouse would lecture

me. Anything but that deadly look of pity. He didn't let me down.

Mouse sank back in his chair, his glasses jumping down his nose, exposing two puffy eyes. 'Your experience proves what I've always said: you're superior to them.'

'Mouse, I ballsed it up. I wore the wrong clothes, got beaten up, laughed at and pitied. So how does that make me superior?'

Mouse shook his head impatiently.

'You tried to lower yourself to their level but you couldn't. Why? I'll tell you why,' he tapped his forehead. 'Intelligence. You've got it, I've got it. But as for those outside – well listen to them!' Yells and screams could be heard.

'They're probably enjoying themselves by stealing someone's trousers. I feel sorry for them. I really do.' He paused to blow vigorously into his handkerchief. Mouse was an athletic nose-blower. 'No, Richard, you are well out of it. Believe me.' He smiled expectantly before concluding his text. 'You're far, far too intelligent for that lot. If brains were dynamite they wouldn't have enough to blow their heads off.'

He waited for me to laugh and agree with him – but I couldn't. Instead, I argued.

'Mouse, we read books but we don't know how to live. They do.'

Mouse's hand smoothed the page of his book. He was steadying himself before hissing. 'They don't know how to live, they're just filling up the spaces in their lives.

Soon they'll be sitting behind cash registers in stiff white uniforms, doing a mindless job for the rest of their lives. But as for you and me . . .' Mouse put his hands in his blazer and leant forward. I knew what was going to happen next. He flicked open his blazer, exposing a collection of handmade, very professional-looking badges, all in red and black.

'Got a new one,' he said proudly, pointing to a badge which said THE SECOND AGE IS DAWNING. According to Mouse, the first age of intelligence had been in the eighteenth century, then mankind slipped into bad ways, but a second age was due any minute. All his badges proclaimed this new era. He spent hours making them.

'Why don't you wear them on the outside?' I queried. 'You only ever flash those badges at me and they're really good.'

'No, no,' said Mouse. 'I don't need to show off my badges. I'm not an exhibitionist. These badges are for me alone. To remind me . . .'

His voice died away, his blazer was quickly fastened. He went on red alert. So did all the other boffins, for invaders approached. And the most dangerous landing force of all – Lads.

Occasionally the Lads came into the library for a good bundle – they threw books around, threw each other against the shelves – the boffins steeled themselves for such an event. But this time the Lads, led by Steve, Danny and a strangely bashful Tim Grant, whipped through the library and converged around our table.

'All right, Mouse?' said Steve. He was one of the few who ever acknowledged Mouse, one of the few who could afford to. Mouse sniffed in reply.

'We want a word, Richard, outside,' Steve continued. I blinked in astonishment.

'Is that all right?' he asked.

'Yeah, sure.' I tried to sound casual, didn't quite make it. I stood up.

'See you later, Mouse,' I said.

In a voice that was barely a whisper he replied, 'Don't go.'

I could scarcely hear him, yet I could hear all too clearly the urgency in his voice. Mouse was begging me not to go, not to cross over from our territory into theirs. 'Won't be long, Mouse,' I said.

But the way Mouse slunk back in his chair, the utterly defeated way he rubbed his hands over his face showed he thought he'd already lost me.

Five minutes later I stood right on the very edge of the school field. It was packed solid, half the school swarmed around me. Strangely enough, none of them seemed surprised to see an alien boffin amongst them. It was as if they all knew why I was there. Or perhaps it was just that Steve was with me.

A crowd circled around us as Steve smiled down at me. 'All right?' He always seemed to be asking me that. I nodded.

Then his tone changed, becoming quite stern.

'What time did you leave the party on Friday?' he asked.

'About eleven o'clock.' I felt as if I was in the jury box giving evidence.

'Kind of early, wasn't it?'

'Mmm.'

'You didn't let anyone know you were leaving, did you? Not even me.'

'You were busy at the time.'

Steve gave his familiar lazy smile, then he addressed the jury of Lads.

'I reckon the Bof – old Richard here – left early because of what someone did when I wasn't around. Is that right?'

How could I answer that? I tried to avoid even looking at Tim Grant. My silence hung in the air until Steve tossed it aside.

'What happened to you was way out of order,' he pronounced. 'You've a right to enjoy yourself without being hassled and picked on.'

I thought of Memphis; hadn't he a right to enjoy himself and hadn't Steve picked on him on Friday? Just this morning I'd heard Katie saying how Memphis still had ring marks – Steve's ring marks – on his face, but I didn't dare mention any of this.

'Anyway, there's someone here who's got something to say,' concluded Steve. As Steve stepped back, Tim Grant stepped forward. They were so in time you'd have thought they'd rehearsed it. And even before Tim Grant started blustering I started cringing.

'I've got to . . . I want to . . . apologise,' he stuttered.

'Louder,' ordered Steve.

'I want to apologise,' he half-shouted, 'for what I did to you on Friday night. Steve says it was out of order. Definitely. I hope my apology is accepted.' His grovelly, whingy voice didn't belong to his face, especially those eyes, all frosted over with hatred. I didn't blame him though. I wouldn't wish this ceremony on anyone – not even him.

'Do you accept my apology?' he asked a trifle impatiently. Far away a bell rang but no-one stirred. In fact, Anna and Ashley had just joined the audience.

'Yes, I accept your apology,' I said, choking back the embarrassment. Steve clapped me on the back.

'Right, lads, shake hands,' called Danny.

We exchanged limp handshakes. Steve was obviously very pleased by it all. Justice had been done. He patted me on the back again and went over to Anna. I wondered what Ashley was thinking as Steve and Anna linked arms but mainly I wondered at the strangeness of it all. For everyone was now copying Steve and patting me on the back as if I was a stray dog they'd just adopted, while Tim Grant leant against the hedge, all by himself and looking rather pathetic.

The second bell, known as the warning bell, went off, my legs twitched. Hard to break the habit of a lifetime. Normally I'd have run as fast as my legs would carry me to avoid being late. And even here, on the furthest outpost of school, I got a few definite twinges. But I fought against them. For the first time ever I'd been accepted. So I wasn't going to ruin it by running away, towards the bell.

Suddenly, Steve held his head sideways, like thrushes do when they're listening for worms. He was listening for worms too, the kind that teach and swot. It was dead quiet over there, everyone had settled down to work. Now it was safe for the Lads – and one lapsed boffin – to make their entrance.

I waddled along, panting slightly and I hoped silently, studying the Lads. They strutted back to school, so cool and unfazed, exactly how I wanted to be. Luckily our next teacher was a supply, a distinctly snooty supply who spent most of the lesson yarning on about her wonderful daughter. For her first lessons the class had been quiet and watchful. But now she was sussed and there was already a loud hum of noise when Steve opened the door. She saw us and tried the sarcasm attack.

'Well, how nice of you to turn up. Good evening, gentlemen – and ladies.'

'And good night to you,' said Steve, giving her a saucy wink.

She stared at him disbelievingly. Then she went into her aggrieved routine.

'This is not the way you enter my classroom. Now before you all sit down, what have you to say to me?'

'What would you like me to say to you?' said Steve, winking.

'Say it now!' she yelled.

'Say what?' yelled back Steve and he grinned at me.

Suddenly, I felt really high, as if I was in on the joke too.

'Excuse me, Miss,' said Danny in a deceptively timid voice. 'But I love it when you get angry. You look so horny.'

The class fell about while Danny gave a little bow. Only Madame Supply was not amused. She started shuffling around on her seat, clucking indignantly and generally giving an excellent impression of a broody hen.

'I've never been spoken to in such a way. Never!'

'Today you got lucky,' said Steve.

While Danny continued his little boy lost routine.

'Did I say something wrong, Miss?' he asked, rolling his eyes.

The class continued cracking up. I could feel Anna laughing on to my hair – or so it seemed. She was laughing really loudly anyhow, especially when Steve spoke. Madame Supply stood up, exclaiming, 'What is happening to the world today? There's no respect any more. In my day we were polite and respectful to our elders. We opened doors for them, let them go first, asked them if there was anything we could do for them.'

We jostled impatiently. We'd been standing in the doorway for about five minutes, while the rest of the class gave loud yawns. But Madame Supply was lost in the past.

'I blame the schools. No discipline any more. I'm just thankful my daughter's at a private school where she cannot be contaminated.'

'Does she go?' asked Steve suddenly. 'Is she horny too?'

Madame Supply let out a furious squawk.

'You vile, disgusting boy. I will not tolerate such language in my classroom. Get out. Get out.'

'All right, keep your wig on,' said a new voice. One that hadn't been heard before. One who'd never spoken up. But now that someone had got so high on the Lad oxygen around him he dared to speak his thoughts aloud and declared – 'If you hate us so much, what are you doing here? No wonder we all mess about. What else is there to do? You just want to yatter on about your daughter, who we're sick of hearing about . . .'

'Both of you, outside now,' she screeched. 'You're going to Mr Weedle. Come on, move.' But her screeching was interrupted by applause. The class were clapping my outburst. They continued clapping Steve and me as we exited. I even copied Danny and gave a little bow and I felt so good, as if I'd over-dosed on Lad oxygen and then Steve said:

'You sure told her,' and there was admiration in his voice, I swear there was and I floated down that corridor.

It was only when I stood outside Weedle's office that my Lad oxygen supply was suddenly cut off. I was being sent to the deputy head. A boffin nightmare.

I became a bit nervous – no, more than that, scared. Especially when Madame Supply plunged out of Weedle's office with an evil smirk on her face. I didn't trust that smirk. What had she told him? What had he promised to do to us? Had I really spoken up like that? Perhaps Steve sensed my anxiety for as we were ushered into Weedle's office he whispered, 'Don't worry, mate, this'll be a doddle.'

Weedle was, of course, known to the whole school as Widdle: a grey, tired, shrivelled man who muttered on about the school's achievements during final assembly and spent the rest of the time confined to his office seeing bad pupils and moany parents.

As we crept into his office I was overpowered by this ghastly smell of polish. It seemed to get into my eyes and under my clothes, making me want to itch it away. It was as if this room had just been fumigated to take away the smell of the decaying figure propped up at his desk. The desk seemed about four sizes too big for him.

The light was dim and sickly and I couldn't see Widdle too clearly. Only his hand seemed alive. It trembled over a piece of paper. I watched its precarious journey until Steve nudged me.

'Answer him then,' he whispered.

Widdle had begun speaking and I hadn't even noticed. I'd been aware of an irate buzz, like a bluebottle with a hangover, but never realized this was the sound of a human. I strained my ears as they do on films when they're trying to make out a dying man's last words. I decoded '. . . poor start to your career. We don't expect a new boy to behave in this way.' New boy? He thinks I'm new. I glanced at Steve. He stifled a laugh, while the irate drone continued '. . . so hurry up and get yourself sorted out. You've only been here – how many days?'

Two bleak eyes were directed at me.

I thought quickly. How many days ago was the bus crash?

'I've been here for seven days.'

'And what's your name?'

'Ricky, Ricky Hodgson.'

Steve stifled another laugh.

'I shall remember that name. I remember the names of all the pupils here.'

His voice started to wither away as if it was drowning in the polish. And I wasn't scared any more. I mean, I used to wet my pants just thinking of old Widdle, but up close he was just an aged stick insect. A stick insect who'd cast giant shadows of fear on to me – but no longer – I saw him clearly now.

Two sets of waiting – and probably irate – parents led Widdle to finally pass sentence on us.

'You will both go now and apologise to Mrs Howard and I hope you know how to apologise.'

Then we were outside, blinking in the daylight. My amazement burst into laughter.

'But is that it – just apologise – is that it?'

Steve nodded, enjoying my surprise.

'But I can't believe it. I mean, when people got sent to him I imagined all sorts of things happening.'

'Like whippings and floggings?' teased Steve. 'Come on,' he started walking in the opposite direction to the classroom.

'Where are we going?'

'The office.'

The boys' loo reeked – sort of the opposite smell to that in Widdle's chamber.

Steve didn't appear to care as he lounged against the wall, quite at home. He offered me a cigarette.

'No thanks. Bit early for me.'

I didn't tell him I thought cigarettes were cancer sticks and really pathetic – especially as he was puffing away so appreciatively on his. Steve smoked on and didn't talk. But it was a relaxed silence as if we were mates or something. The bell went.

'Give it another two minutes then we'll go and see her.' Steve grinned. 'Just as her next class is arriving, cause her a bit more grief.' He stubbed his cigarette out, pressing down harder than he needed. 'She's a snooty cow. You ever seen her breezing down the corridor, banging past anyone who gets in her way?'

'Then afterwards,' I added eagerly, 'she looks back down the corridor to see how many people she's hacked off.'

'What a cow.' Steve spat right on to his dead cigarette.

And I suddenly realised how much he hated her. She wasn't just a bad teacher, she was an enemy. I wondered how many other teachers Steve saw as enemies. Then Steve suddenly peered right at me like he was inspecting me.

'What's with the Ricky stuff?'

'It's my name – the name I'd like to be called.'

I shuffled about uncomfortably. 'I hate being called Boffin.' Steve nodded while he lit up another cigarette.

'That bus crash, do you still think about it?'

'Yes, a lot,' I answered truthfully.

'That was bad,' he puffed thoughtfully. 'I read about it in the local paper. They didn't describe it as well as you, though.' Then he carried on smoking and observing me, as if he was really trying to figure me out, until he said in his drawl-like way, 'The bus you were on, crashing, is that the reason you're acting different now?'

'Yeah. It made me realise you've only got one life and . . .' I didn't quite know what I was trying to say. I wondered if Steve did, for he suddenly changed the subject.

'Those trousers you're wearing. They your only ones?'

'No, no. They just look the same.'

'Used to really bug me – you always wearing the same trousers,' he laughed. White cold waves of embarrassment ran up and down my back. But then his expression changed again.

'I'll help you. Help you get some decent clothes. Think I know what would suit you. Make you look the business.'

I couldn't believe my luck.

'Oh Steve, thanks, that's great,' I enthused.

'No sweat. And you can come up The Fleur with us on Friday, if you like.'

Me going up the pub with the Lads, with Steve. I could only gape in amazement – and joy.

He strolled to the door, cigarette still perched in his mouth.

'Come on, I can hear her class arriving. Let's wind her up.' But before he left he tapped the wall, 'And we'll put an end to these.' He was pointing at a 'SAVE THE BOFFIN' picture scrawled above the light switch.

I looked. And for the first time I could look at a 'SAVE THE BOFFIN' sketch without the usual feelings of shame and personal affront. It was as if I'd already shed my boffin skin and left that part of my life far behind me.

That night I was too dazed to dream, for real life had suddenly overtaken my dreams. In one day my life had turned about and now with Steve helping me, who knew how many great things lay ahead?

Welcome to Thrillsville

'I've been waiting for you.'

Words to strike terror into the soul when spoken by my mum. Had she found out my savings book was missing? She'd have a blue fit when she discovered I'd now spent two hundred pounds of my savings on new clothes. But her tone was cheerful, almost playful, as she said: 'Come on, Nip, close your eyes.'

I obeyed, heard some rustling and opened my eyes to behold . . .

'You thought I'd forgotten, didn't you?' she cooed. 'But see, I remembered you wanted new clothes and today I saw this young man in the library wearing such a smart shirt and I thought – Richard would like that. So I asked the boy – such a nice polite boy too – if he'd mind telling me where he'd bought the shirt. And do you know where he bought it?'

I'd have guessed a joke-shop! Not even in my bleakest boffin days would I have willingly squeezed that over my stomach. But Mum didn't wait for me to reply. 'I went all round Wycombe to find the shop, a special man's shop. A man's shop,' she repeated, searching my face for the expected response of, 'Wow, not a *man's* shop!'

'You shouldn't have bothered, Mum,' I said. 'I don't deserve that shirt.'

Mum smiled triumphantly. 'I won't tell you the price but yes, it was expensive. Worth it though, every penny. And it'll make you look quite the young executive.'

It was as bad as that.

'I'm sure Ashley will be impressed by her distinguished, handsome young partner.'

You see, there's no way I could have told Mum I was going up the pub tonight, so I'd told her I was going out for a meal with some friends. Mum, of course, assumed there was just one friend going, Ashley, and she imagined Ashley and me having a romantic candlelit dinner for two. I let Mum think that; kept her happy.

'You are still going out with Ashley?' Mum smiled mischievously. 'You're not going to get cold feet this time are you, like before?'

'Oh Mum.'

'Poor Sarah.'

'Mum, I was four years old.'

It was too late. Mum had already gone into an 'I remember it well' trance. Nothing could stop the whole event being brought to life yet again.

'I said to you, "Would you like to go and play with a dear little soul called Sarah?" And you said "Oh yes please," but of course you thought I was going to be there too. So I left you with Sarah's mother – a very nice woman – while I did my hours at the paper shop. Well I'd scarcely got inside the house again when there was this frantic knocking at the door. And there you were with Sarah's mother, who was saying, "I'm sorry, Mrs Hodgson, but the whole time you've been away, Richard has been distraught. Absolutely distraught." And I looked down at your little face and it was all red and swollen from crying. And do you remember what you said?'

I nodded grimly.

'You said, "I'll be good, Mum, please don't send me away again." And the next day I handed in my notice at the paper shop. What's a few coppers compared with your children's welfare?'

Mum rocked back and forth, warming herself on the memory while I waited patiently. There was no point in interrupting her when she was on one of her story-telling binges, you just had to let things run their course. Gradually she returned to the present.

'I know you're going out for a meal later – but you need something warm inside you before you go so I've heated up a pork pie with some chips and mushy peas and there's a slice of bread pudding for afters if you're still hungry, which I expect you will be.' Her voice softened, 'Pleased with your new shirt then?'

'It's great, Mum.'

A comet of joy shot across her face. 'I knew you'd like it.'

I felt quite guilty depositing Mum's shirt under that seat on the common. I folded it carefully first. Poor old Mum, she had tried and it was good of her to care, especially as Kay was coming over this weekend and Mum seemed to be worried. But that shirt, it was so old fashioned, it was pre-boffin. I cast off Mum's shirt and plunged into the clothes Steve had selected for me. He'd picked them out so quickly too. 'This is your image,' he'd said. I didn't argue.

To my relief Steve was waiting for me, outside The Fleur, just as he'd promised. He'd been lounging against the wall, chatting to a couple of girls. As soon as I appeared the girls sloped off while Steve walked round me as if I was some sort of exhibit, then he let out a low whistle of appreciation.

'You're safe, well safe.'

I grinned proudly.

'One thing,' Steve became my coach. 'When you walk in there, don't rush at it.'

I nodded solemnly, praying I wouldn't let Steve down.

Steve glanced furtively around him. 'There's no-one about for a minute. Have a quick practice. Stroll up to that wall.'

I moved about a millionth of a centimetre.

'No, no, too springy. Don't bounce along like that. Look, watch me.' He did his famous glide-strut.

'I could practise for ever and never copy that.'

'Yes you can, just . . .'

'All right, Steve?' a voice called out of the darkness. Steve nodded, then said to me, 'No time. We'd better go in. Just walk in as though you're the coolest thing to hit town.'

He made it sound so easy. He sauntered towards the pub before suddenly turning back, lowering his voice as if he was about to give me a secret password.

'Meant to tell you. Tim Grant won't be up tonight. That's definite. Does that give you a boost?'

I nodded. I had been worried about Tim Grant causing me grief tonight and yet, the way Steve had said about Tim Grant not coming up, all this 'that's definite' stuff was a bit chilling. It was as if Steve was pulling all our strings. He could bring me on stage – and yet he could also cut off Tim Grant's strings. That's what he'd done. Suddenly Tim Grant was out and I was in, but for how long? Not long, I feared.

As soon as we entered the pub all Steve's instructions fell out of my mind. It took all my concentration just keeping up with him. For already it was crammed full of people, many from our school. Of course, Steve flowed through them while I tried to lumber around them, saying, 'Excuse me,' but I don't think anyone heard me.

'I thought you'd gone back home,' said Steve, leaning nonchalantly against the bar as I finally joined him.

'No, no,' I panted. 'It just took me longer to get through.'

I checked my wallet. Mum had warned me about

pickpockets. Then finding it still there, I asked, 'What would you like to drink?'

'It's all right, I've got ours – and Danny's. There we go, Carol.'

A pretty dark-haired girl behind the bar smiled at Steve, the way girls normally smile at Steve.

'Carol, meet my mate Ricky.'

She looked at me with all the interest you might shower on a stale mushroom.

Steve added, 'This was the guy who was in that bus crash last week. The one that went through the hairdresser's.'

'Oh, I heard about that. A friend of mine was offered a job there. Nearly took it too.' She gazed at me again, distinctly impressed now.

'I bet you'll never forget the moment when it all happened.'

'No,' I said gravely.

'He might tell you all about it later, Carol.' Then he thrust a pint of lager in my hand and edged me away, murmuring, 'Could be in there, Ricky.'

But I think he was joking.

I examined the pint. 'You bought me all this, Steve?'

'Yeah, you'll soon get that down you. Ever drunk lager before?'

'No, no, sometimes Dad gives me a sip out of his can of beer and at Christmas I have a glass of sherry . . .'

'Yeah, well, I'd keep quiet about that if I were you. Better join Danny.'

Following Steve this time was a bit like taking part in an assault course. As before, Steve darted ahead while I tried to manoeuvre myself and my pint around everyone. I was concentrating so hard I didn't notice this other guy bound alongside me. Our pint glasses knocked, flinging half his drink on the ground, while my pint remained more or less intact.

'I'm awfully sorry,' I cried. 'Let me give you the money for another pint.' He glared down at me. He was very big and very angry.

'I wanted that one,' he yelled.

'Lick it up then,' said Steve.

To my great relief Steve was there behind me.

'And put your money away, Ricky, it was as much his fault as yours. Wasn't it, Jonesy?'

The guy grunted and then disappeared into the crowd.

'Can't leave you alone for a minute,' teased Steve, 'without you getting into a fight.'

'It was that guy,' I said. 'He seemed really mad.'

'Oh he's all right. Bit of a laugh sometimes.'

Steve stayed with me now, guiding me towards our table. Danny and some other guys from my year all did exaggerated double-takes when they saw me.

'This is a new guy, Ricky,' said Steve.

'All right, Ricky,' Danny edged a space for me. 'Take a pew.'

'Welcome to Thrillsville,' Danny continued half sarcastically.

'What do you think of it then?' asked Steve, as if I'd just stepped into his home.

I stared around me incredulously. 'To think of all this going on, right on my doorstep, it's incredible.' I stiffened. My boffin antennae told me I was being watched. I followed my instincts. A guy in a white poloneck was staring at me. His eyes were like slits. He didn't look friendly.

'Who's that?' I asked.

Steve lowered his voice, 'Don't worry, that's Big Mick He thinks he's the hard guy here and he checks out any new faces.'

I was terrified and curious. I looked at that strange face again.

'No, don't eyeball him, Ricky,' said Steve warningly. 'He'll think you want trouble and he's not a guy to tangle with.'

I immediately stared intently at my drink.

'He's just put his brother in hospital,' continued Danny. 'They were arguing over whose turn it was to make the tea.'

'All right, all right,' said Steve, perhaps seeing me shivering. 'Try your lager, Ricky.'

'Down in one,' called out one of the guys round the table. 'Only joking,' he added, after a warning glance from Steve.

All eyes were on me as I took a sip.

'Don't sip it,' whispered Steve.

I took a longer swig, like I'd seen them do on television. It tasted revolting, really bitter and horrible.

'How does it taste?' asked Danny.

'Great,' I lied.

'Get it down you, then,' said Steve.

That was an order. So I drank it how you'd drink medicine, very quickly so you don't get the taste.

'Look at Bof downing the lager,' said Danny. 'He's going to be a right old boozer.' He said it admiringly.

I decided to finish the pint. Get this part of the initiation over. As I finished it I smacked my lips appreciatively – thought that was quite a good touch. I looked across at Steve. He was smiling proudly. His protégé had passed the first round.

'Good evening, boys,' said an adult voice.

I started. Everyone in this pub was young, except for this guy. He was really old and shrunken and on the cadge.

'Just came to tell you, your young ladies are on the horizon.'

They laughed at him, friendly, yet patronising.

'Cheers for telling us, Paddy – we're ready for 'em,' and Danny winked at him.

Paddy winked back. 'And could any of you young men be buying a poor old man a drink?'

He looked at Steve, who handed him a couple of pounds.

'One drink, Paddy, that's all.'

He bent forward. He stank. 'You're grand lads – and I'll tell your girls that you are waiting here with your tongues hanging out.' He gave another elaborate wink, then went off, fingering his coins and sniggering to himself.

'You gonna get lucky tonight, Danny?' asked Steve.

'When don't I get lucky?' said Danny.

'The girls like a bit of black, don't they?' said Steve.

Danny sat back, grinning broadly. 'We're the best – ask any girl around here. Give Anna one for me, Steve.'

Now Steve was grinning away and I could sense all the Lads drawing together. So tonight, Steve was going to give Anna 'one'.

I could imagine the process really clearly: they'd be sprawled over each other and they'd move in slow motion and there'd be soft, warm lighting and a Motown soundtrack . . .

'What about you, Ricky – you going to get lucky?' said Danny, smiling.

'Yes, sure,' I nodded.

Actually, I'd never thought of it. The girl who fancied me hadn't been created yet.

'Who's the lucky girl?' asked Danny, grinning away.

'Ashley,' I said. That was the first name that came into my head. 'Is she up tonight?' I added.

'Ashley's always up someone,' quipped Danny.

'The only time Ash says no is when you ask her if she's had enough. She's been up so many guys she should carry a government health warning . . .'

I couldn't identify who was saying what. Everyone was talking at once, all giving with jokes that had one punchline – Ashley equals Slag. I couldn't even pretend to laugh. You can't when you've been reduced to a joke yourself. I didn't so much feel sorry for Ashley as identify with her.

So I said, 'I like Ashley.' I hadn't intended to shout. But everyone heard and stopped joking and misunderstood.

I didn't mean 'like' as they meant. I hardly knew her really.

But Steve was going, 'We'll help you get inside Ash's knickers, won't we, lads?' And he seemed really chuffed about me wanting to 'give one' to his ex-girlfriend. Everyone did. Unwittingly, I'd scored more points.

'So what's funny?' Anna shimmered before us.

She was wearing a track suit top that belonged to Steve and this ring on a chain round her neck which she kept touching. Even I guessed whose ring it was. She sat down next to Steve. Everyone automatically moved. She bestowed a smile on Danny.

'Saw your sister outside.'

He looked angry.

'She'd better stay outside,' he began. Then he put on his usual Danny grin again. 'She's a silly cow,' he said.

Next, Anna honoured me with a glance. 'You look great.' She turned to Steve. 'You've done a good job.'

Then suddenly, they kissed. A proper tongue kiss. And again. I watched, fascinated. They didn't seem at all self-conscious about performing before an audience. Then, just as suddenly, the kissing stopped – or paused – and Anna was addressing us.

'Ash is just coming. When you see her, you've got to like her hair, all right?'

'What's it like?' asked Danny.

'Well, it's very nice,' said Anna, smirking as she said it.

Ashley came into view. There were gasps. Her blonde hair was now a violent purple.

She plonked two drinks on the table, gave Anna a mock curtsey as she said, 'Your G & T, ma'am,' then hugged Steve very hard. 'Hello, babe,' she cried.

He hugged her back, then put his arm tightly around Anna. Obviously embarrassed, Ashley faltered for a moment before hugging Danny.

'Hiya, babe.'

She hugged all the other blokes at the table, except me. I was quite disappointed. She did give me a big smile though as she said, 'You look brilliant, absolutely brilliant.'

Then, having greeted everyone, Ashley stood rather uncertainly in front of us.

No-one invited her to sit down. So I stood up.

'Would you like a seat?' I said it rather badly as if she was some little old lady on the bus. But she flushed with pleasure.

'Oh, that's sweet of you.'

'Very sweet,' murmured Anna.

'But I'm fine here, thanks.'

Another heavy silence as Anna and Steve resumed their squishy kisses.

Danny remarked conversationally, 'What's with your hair, Ash?'

'I thought I'd have a change. Got bored with the old colour. It was supposed to be burgundy, that's what it said on the box.' She was speaking to Danny but her eyes never left Anna and Steve. I felt really sorry for her.

But I couldn't blame Steve.

'How about flashing the fags, Steve?' asked Danny.

Cigarettes were passed round – one came to me.

'No thanks,' I murmured. I didn't want to get into smoking.

'Go on, go on,' urged Steve.

'Oh, don't make him if he doesn't want to,' said Anna. 'I don't smoke, so why should he?'

'Because he's a man,' interrupted Danny. 'Go on, Ricky, won't do you any harm to try one.'

I looked at Steve. He was willing me to say 'Yes'. So I said, 'Yes.'

'I'll light it for you.'

He placed the lit cigarette in my hand. The whole table was watching me avidly as if I was going to do a trick with this cigarette or something. I took my face to the cigarette. I held the cigarette tightly between my lips and sucked.

'If you suck it, you don't get any of it,' said Steve. 'Inhale, then take it down.'

I breathed in, took a big gulp and proceeded to cough my guts up. There was some laughing but it wasn't unkind laughing, everyone was keen to help. So they fired instructions at me while I carried on coughing. I was getting a bit scared actually. When I finally stopped coughing, Steve snatched my cigarette away.

'Look, watch me, Ricky.'

He put it in his mouth, then whipped it out again.

'You've been bum-sucking this.' He wiped my spit off and said, 'Now watch this, Ricky.'

I knew he was eager for me to get it right so I watched carefully, even though I dreaded doing it again.

'See, I take a deep lug, take it down, only I don't swallow, I take it through my nose.'

I took the cigarette from him.

'Away you go, Ricky,' said Danny. He was cheering me on. They all were as I tried again. I proceeded to have a second coughing fit. And a third.

'Keep going,' said Steve. He wasn't smiling now.

The fourth time I had an idea. After taking a 'lug' I kept the smoke in my mouth for a few seconds, let them think I'd taken it down, then blew it out. There were cheers. I repeated my trick. More cheers, while I felt really dizzy and strange. It was as if I'd been running for a long time, leaving me with this tingly, tickly feeling in my insides. But I'd done it. I'd smoked my way into Ladhood.

Danny clapped me on the back. 'You've done really great, and just for that I'm going to buy you a pint.'

One hour, two and a half pints later I was, as they say, out of my head. In fact my head had long since gone and the rest was just cotton wool. I felt so woozy and light, that any minute I could be floating out of my fat carcase, far, far away. And best of all, I didn't care any more. All my shyness had been blown away.

I scanned the scene, a line of pints beside me, all gifts, and layers of people around our table blocking out all those other sweating people jostling for space. Nothing could block out this strange aroma though – a cross between really strong after-shave and really stale beer.

'Are you still enjoying yourself?' asked Steve.

I tried to get him into focus. Couldn't quite. But it's easier talking to people when they're out of focus.

'Me, enjoying myself? Yes, I'm great. It's wicked here. Nothing like my house.'

As I spoke I could hear my voice really clearly, as if I was listening to myself on a tape-recorder.

'What's your house like?' asked Steve. 'You live down . . .'

'My house,' I interrupted, 'is like a morgue with a juke-box. Only I haven't got a juke-box.

Heads were bobbing in my direction. I must be talking very loudly. But around me, ripples of laughter and attention.

'What would you normally be doing tonight?' asked a glittering blur that could only be Anna. She spoke to me as if I was from another country.

'I sit at home, watch the telly. I know the times of every television programme. And I read. And my mum knits things for babies and my dad snoozes. And sometimes, as a variation, he farts. After a fart he says, "How do you do?" and Mum gets annoyed and opens the doors – and that's really exciting.'

'How about pets?' asked Anna.

This was turning into an interview. My first.

'I had a pet duck. It drowned.' More laughter. I drew closer to the laughter.

'Got a girlfriend?' asked Anna.

More laughter before I'd even answered.

'I'm looking for one,' I called back, my voice growing louder with each answer. 'Trouble is, I've got a funny body.'

'Oh no you haven't,' cried Ashley.

'Oh yes I have. And as for my face: my eyes are like two overdone fried eggs and my eyebrows are usually only seen in horror films on someone who's about to turn into a wolf. I tried to grow a moustache – but nothing grows in the shade of that nose. I tell you, my best side is round the back of my head.' The Boffin had become a stand-up comic. It seemed like half the pub was rocking with laughter.

'Listen, lads.' An elderly interruption.

'You've had your drink, Paddy,' said Steve quickly and he was all set to turn back to my cabaret turn. But Paddy said in a low but insistent whisper—

'It's not your money I want. I'm about to do you a good turn. The pigs are outside. There's going to be a raid.'

I started to laugh at Paddy and his talk of raids. After all, drinking isn't illegal. I'd totally forgotten that it was me who was illegal.

But then I noticed how dented the atmosphere had become and that everyone was standing up, whitefaced, anxious, under-age.

'My dad said if I got caught he'd leave me in the cell all night and it would serve me right,' said Ashley.

'They won't lock us up,' snapped Anna, 'just take our

90

names and – I'm lucky, my mum thinks things like this are quite funny,' her voice faded away. Fear was fluttering over everyone. Except Steve.

'Stop gabbing and get moving,' he ordered. 'The pigs aren't in yet,' he patted Paddy on the back. 'We owe you one, Paddy.'

'That you do, lads – a double pint.'

'We'll make it a triple,' replied Steve, then to me, 'Move it now, Ricky, you've got to keep up.'

And this time I did keep up, using my weight to steamroller my way through the masses of sweaty blurs. Only, where were we going? For Steve was leading us away from the entrance.

'Where are we going?' I asked Danny's neck.

'The loos,' he replied.

My exclamation of surprise was drowned by an almighty yell. All eight of us fell back on each other.

'We're too late,' cried Ashley. 'They're in.'

Steve held his head sideways, as I'd seen him on the back field.

'We're all right. Been a big win on the machines, that's all. Shift it, Danny.'

But Danny wasn't shifting. Instead, he said in a low, choking voice, 'My sister's over there, stupid cow.'

'That's tough,' said Steve, pushing Danny towards the loo, 'but there's no time to get her.'

'I can't leave her,' said Danny, and before anyone could reply he was ploughing his way through the crowd. Soon he was lost behind a haze of bodies and smoke.

I could sense Steve wavering before he said, 'Move it. We haven't got much time.'

Anna whispered, 'See you outside,' as she and Ashley slipped into the girls' loo while I was half-pushed into the boys.

'Boffin,' cried a couple of third years in there, when they saw me.

'Out!' ordered Steve, as if he was in charge of the loos. They didn't argue. Steve sprinted to the window. It was wide open.

'Okay, Ricky, we're piling out through the window. You first.'

'Shouldn't he go last,' said a voice behind me, 'because he'll take the longest?'

There were murmurs of agreement.

'No, because if he's caught in here it'll be harder on him than any of us,' said Steve briskly.

'I don't mind going last,' I began. I'd have preferred it in a way.

'No, you're going out now.'

The loo door opened. 'Get lost,' said Steve.

It quickly shut again.

My eyes swivelled upwards. 'It's quite high,' I faltered.

'I'll give you a leg up.'

He cupped his hands together. 'Put your foot in there.'

My stomach gave a sudden violent jump. I didn't think I could do this. Especially with an audience. An impatient audience. I can never vault over those boxes in PE, no matter how many 'goes' I have.

'Are you sure somebody else wouldn't like . . .'

'No,' barked Steve. 'Hurry up,' then rather more gently, 'You can do it.' I placed my foot in the cupped hands. And suddenly, I was up in the air. Steve had, single-handed, hoisted me up. 'Now hold on to the window.'

I did that.

'Now push yourself through,' said Steve.

'How do I do that?' I squeaked.

'Just wiggle your weight through,' said Steve. 'It's easy.'

At that moment I hated Steve.

'Kick your legs up,' he continued.

'Only, don't kick 'em too much, one guy went through the window doing that,' called someone.

'Shut up,' said Steve. 'I'll give you a push – we all will.'

They all pushed on my bum, some calling out, 'Heave!' while I let out a yell of pain. I was hanging there, half inside half outside. The frame went right through the middle of my stomach like a knife.

'Keep going,' said Steve, 'come down hands first.'

Then a voice said, 'It's all right, I've got him.'

Ashley had one of my hands, Anna the other, and suddenly I was out of the window, landing with a mighty splat. The contents of a dustbin fell alongside me. So did Ashley and Anna.

I heaved myself into a sitting position. Something dark and dung-like had landed on my leg. I flipped it away. It was the remains of a meat-pie. I shook myself and saw Ashley and Anna doing the same.

'I'm really sorry,' I stuttered. But luckily, they were both laughing. 'Poor old Boffin, what an experience for you,' cried Ashley.

And I didn't feel light and airy any more, but my usual clumsy, gross self. Especially when I watched the boys pile out of the window like goods coming off a conveyor belt, still laughing about my belly-flop out the window. But again Steve silenced them all and the commander became a commando as he slowly crouched at a look-out post. Then he ran back to us.

'Pigs swarming everywhere. My brother reckoned they were out to close this pub and that's how they'll do it, by catching all the under-age drinkers. So, until they're inside, we'd better get behind these bins.'

No-one moved.

'Move it, unless you all want to end up down the nick.'

Rather surprisingly, Anna led the way. We followed.

Ashley and I shared a bin. She giggled as she took a particle of congealed meat pie out of my hair and I suddenly thought if Mum could see me now, she'd never believe it. Poor Mum will be picturing me in some swanky restaurant having a candlelit dinner with Ashley, not kneeling beside a dustbin, with her taking two-year-old meat-pie out of my hair.

There was some whispering. 'Cool it,' ordered Steve and not a moment too soon. For above our heads some-one was fiddling with a window. 'It does lock,' he said. The voice could only belong to a policeman. And then there was that awful, swelling quiet, which I prayed wouldn't burst. Just one movement on my part and that torch could come homing down on me, on everyone.

What was he doing there? Ashley and I exchanged tense smiles. If he does sight anyone, don't let it be me. I could stand anything, even a night in the cells, provided I wasn't the one who gave us away.

The silence stretched. Any second now it was going to snap. And then it did, with the window being pulled tight and locked – and us legging it like crazy to the common.

On the common everyone splayed themselves over the grass, panting with relief. Except for Steve.

Anna touched his shoulder, 'We're all right now,' she said.

'Danny,' said Steve quickly.

To my shame I'd momentarily forgotten about Danny, trapped inside the pub with his sister. Perhaps even now being rounded up.

'His parents will go ape,' said Steve.

Everyone nodded sympathetically.

'I shouldn't have let Danny go on his own,' said Steve.

'You couldn't have left us,' argued Anna.

'I let him down,' pronounced Steve firmly.

Steve's words seemed to be swirled up in the air as the wind beat around us, bouncing the litter into the air and carrying towards us, a call, 'Steve!' A voice that sounded just like Danny. Steve stared disbelievingly at us as if we'd conjured up the voice. And then he listened again and yelled, 'He's out, the jammy sod is out!' He yelled again when the jammy sod and his sister sprinted towards us. We all cheered as Steve ran around him, his eyes glistening like ice. 'How did you manage it?' he exclaimed.

Danny flung himself on the ground, while his sister Sherrone stood a little way from us, obviously very embarrassed. I'd seen her round school. She was only fourteen but already really striking looking.

'We were so lucky,' Danny began, then he had to stop. He still hadn't caught his breath.

Then Danny started again. 'Just as the pigs came in, there was this massive fight. Big Mick went for Jim Kemp.'

'What a grin,' interrupted Steve.

Danny nodded then gasped on. 'Big Mick reckons Kempie had been eye-balling his girl. So there's this almighty punch-up just as the pigs pile in. Of course, the pigs all dive-bombed into the fight while Sis and I scarpered out double-quick.' He banged his fists on to the grass. 'We were so lucky . . . so lucky. If Sis and I had got done by the police I reckon my dad would have disowned us, shipped us back to Jamaica anyhow. So lucky.'

He kept chanting that phrase until Steve made as if to hug him, then turned the hug into a friendly fight.

They were both so relieved. And that was what amazed and impressed me. Steve was as relieved as Danny about his lucky escape. In fact, Steve was drenched with relief.

He and Danny were real best mates, whereas Mouse

and me – we enjoyed each other's company, but there were definite limits to our friendship. Limits that Steve and Danny had gone far, far beyond.

It was dark and cold now and my stomach felt as if half of it had been sliced off by the window frame in that loo. It was all sore and hollow and yet none of that mattered, especially when Danny said to me. 'You've done really well tonight.' And beside him was Steve, beaming proudly. And right then I knew I'd slipped up the ranks. I didn't quite know what I was now but I wasn't a boffin any more.

Steve said, 'We're stepping out to a night club. So come along, Ricky, should be a good ruse.'

I marvelled at their energy even while I knew my body could just make it home.

'I'd like to,' I said, 'but my stomach has other ideas.'

Steve nodded sympathetically.

'You've done a lot tonight. Still, you are very welcome.'

'Welcome where?' asked Ashley, slipping alongside Steve.

'Er ... we might go to a night club,' said Steve abruptly.

'Tiffany's?' she asked.

'Yeah.'

'Supposed to be good there,' she said.

'Supposed to be.'

Both Danny and Steve laughed uneasily. And I was hoping Ashley would walk away. But she didn't. Instead, she laughed, rubbed Steve's shoulder and whispered,

'Room for one more?' That same piercingly light tone.

'Afraid not,' said Steve.

At least he was embarrassed as he went on, 'We're going in my brother's car, and there's already me, Danny, and Anna going with him and his girlfriend. So I don't think there'll be room, will there?'

'No, sorry,' said a new voice. The voice sounded regretful. But I noticed that as she spoke, Anna fastened her arm around Steve. She was securing her property against all intruders while Ashley backed away guiltily. She'd tried to re-claim Steve twice, thrown herself full-pelt at him, and been thrown quickly back. And watching her edging away from us was agony. I could taste her hurt and humiliation and I knew she was frantically trying to disappear into the background, only that purple hair kept jutting out like some ghastly eyesore. There was nowhere for Ashley to hide.

I couldn't just leave her squirming and twitching like some bewildered animal suddenly caught up in a car's headlights, could I? So I called out, 'Do you want to walk home with me, Ashley?' Everyone heard and made the usual 'Oooh!' noises and a smile jerked across Ashley's face while Danny goes, 'There's no stopping him.'

Steve resumed his coach role.

'She's a good one to start on, Ricky. Lots of experience. No need for any chat-up lines.'

When Ashley linked my arm, there were more cheers and she leant against me as if she fancied me although I knew this was for Steve's benefit – well, mainly for Steve's benefit. But Steve didn't seem at all bothered. Instead he patted me on the back declaring, 'You've had a good night, Ricky, and it's not over yet.'

A Fuse Any Second

It sounded weird – the sound of a girl alongside me. To someone who'd only ever been accompanied by the dull thud of Mum's sensible shoes, the very fast, very urgent tapping of Ashley's high heels was a most exciting change.

And she was so funny. I mean, she was telling stories about her sisters – she's got three of them – and they weren't that funny but she had this giggle in her voice that was infectious. So I was laughing at her stories, without quite knowing why. And everything I asked her she turned into stories. Not that I asked her about Anna and Steve. I couldn't imagine even Ashley being able to joke tonight's humiliation away.

We were turning off this twisty, hilly road by her estate when I spotted a crew of Year Nine boys all doing their 'we're men now' walk. I smiled vaguely until I sighted their leader.

He had this black scarf right over his face. Only his

eyes were visible. But I'd know his look of piercing hatred anywhere.

So much had happened tonight – and I'd moved so far forward – that seeing Tim Grant now was like seeing a figure from my past. This time, though, there was to be no cowering before his evil eye. I'd got to face up to him. I thought of Steve, he'd given me some advice about standing up for myself. What was it? Oh yes: if you feel awkward and uneasy, bung your thumbs through your belt-loop – he'd called it the fully operational, twiddling position. So I twiddled, while Ashley pointed a bit of conversation Tim Grant's way.

'Tim, how are you, babe? I thought it was you.'

'Well, you were right, it was me, is me.'

There was a rather awkward pause as he pulled down his scarf. They both seemed oddly nervous.

'Been to your body-building class then?' she asked.

'That's right. You've got to keep testing yourself, go on beating the pain barrier.'

'Still keeping the charts?'

He flexed his arms the way they do on body-building displays. 'Fifteen and a half inches now. When you went out with me it was eleven.'

I flinched. Ashley had been out with him. Surely not. He kept his arm flexed in front of her nose until she quipped, 'Even your muscles are going to have muscles soon,' but she sounded more patronising than impressed.

'Anyway, Ash, got to move the lads on.' Then, with fake casualness, 'Have a good time tonight, did you?'

'Until the pigs arrived, big raid up The Fleur.'

'Not again, there's too many of these pig raids,' he laughed mirthlessly. 'The pigs stopped us tonight. Wanted to know where we were going, obviously thought we looked trouble.'

His supporters grinned proudly.

'Mind you, pigs are often stopping me. Get sick of it. Anyway, Ash, sorry and all about your bit of hassle.' He darted a glance of undiluted hatred in my direction. I remembered something else Steve told me: whenever anyone talks to you don't look at them all the time. Instead, every so often look over them, out the window or whatever, that prevents them feeling too important and keeps them in their place. So right then I started staring intently over Tim Grant's head. Out of the corner of my eye I could see his mouth all hung open as if he was waiting to strike. But then, he pulled his scarf up higher than before and led off his troupe of thirteen-year-old body-builders.

'Poor old Grantie,' sighed Ashley. 'Poor old Grantie.'

Her sympathy infuriated me.

'Poor nothing, he's a bully,' I snapped.

'He's not all bad,' she said, her shoes tapping briskly beside me.

'Yes he is, a total bully.'

'No, no, he's not really. I should know. I used to go out with him.'

The more she defended him, the more she stoked up my anger. There's nothing worse than being told your worst enemy is really a nice guy. 'I can't believe you went out with him,' I said, adding rudely, 'you must have been really desperate.'

Ashley didn't take offence, instead she said cheerily – 'Yes, I was. Very desperate. I'd bought these two tickets for a really good disco in Aylesbury thinking someone's bound to ask me and I'll have the tickets all ready. Only no-one did,' she laughed. 'So I ended up having to go round knocking on doors offering myself, and my tickets. Finally, I got down to Grantie,' her voice softened, 'and during the evening he was so nice, but all I wanted was for him to escort me in. I didn't fancy him or anything. But when the disco ended Grantie came back over to me and asked me out. I said, "Thank you, but I don't think so," trying to be tactful. But then he said he wouldn't leave until I did go out with him. He meant it too. So in the end I gave in and we went out just once. He spent the whole evening talking about body-building and how his muscles are going to sprout out like Danny's.'

Her story had fascinated and annoyed me. But I didn't want to be made to feel sympathy for someone who'd caused me so much hassle. Almost as if she could read my thoughts, Ashley said, 'What Grantie did to you at my party was wrong, awful. Everyone had a real go at him about it. I did, especially.'

'I was pretty annoyed too,' I said dryly.

'But in a way it was a compliment to you.'

'Pardon?'

'Look, you've got more than a bit of savvy upstairs. Surely you can see that Steve has been Grantie's protector, always looking out for him, making him one of the team. Then suddenly you come on the scene and Grantie's slung out and you're in his place.'

I shivered. 'I'm not in his place. I'm nothing to do with him.'

'No, but tonight, for example, he'd normally . . .'

'I'm nothing to do with him,' I repeated. 'You talk like I'm a substitute for him, but I'm not. I'm totally different. I . . .' My voice was shaking. My whole body was shaking as it fought down a terror that threatened to take my breath away. But the terror defeated me, leaving me gasping furiously. I tried to get my breath. Ashley leant over me. I waved her away, flinging myself down by the wall.

'I didn't mean to upset you,' she cried, crouching beside me.

I shook my head, trying to say it wasn't her fault. But I couldn't utter anything except for a few desperate sounds. I knew those sounds well. For when I was young I had asthma attacks all the time. Now they only seized me occasionally. Every stage of the attack was familiar – and still terrifying. The terror subsided. I managed to cry, 'Asthma, that's all, very mild asthma.'

'Thank God you're all right. You went purple.'

I could feel Ashley's hair brushing against the side of my lips. See her stricken face in sudden close-up. I was enjoying her concern until I saw my stomach leering up at me. In an effort to help me breathe, Ashley'd undone so many buttons she'd unveiled layers of my pinky-white flab.

'Not a pretty sight,' I said, scrambling to my feet and doing myself up. 'I'm sorry you had to witness me in that state.'

'Don't be silly. It was all my fault mentioning Tim Grant, you've every reason . . .'

Ashley's road stretched ahead.

'Come back to my place for a coffee?' she asked.

'Oh well.' I hadn't expected this.

'Oh come on. You can see my own special room. And anyhow, I can't just leave you after one of your attacks. You might have another one.'

That was exactly what I feared and if it did recur I wanted it to be in private. But she was most insistent. So I followed Ashley into a large shed in her back garden. She said, 'This is where I come if I want to make a noise or entertain friends.' Her use of the word 'friends' gave me a tingle of pleasure.

The shed was musty and messy and cosy.

'Sit down anywhere,' called Ashley, filling a kettle.

I gazed around me. There were no seats, just piles of records and pop magazines – and two striped camp beds.

I sat gingerly on the middle of one. Camp beds have a habit of seizing up on me. They're also always too narrow. Ashley flung what looked like a pile of sketch pads into the centre of the room – crying – 'This place is a tip, but who cares. I like it messy.'

'So do I, homely.'

'Lie right out, then. You look like you're waiting for an interview.'

I very slowly sank back on the camp bed. It creaked and groaned but I didn't blame it.

'How are you feeling now?' she asked.

'A bit fragile.'

'You wait until you've had my coffee. How do you like it?'

'As it comes.'

Five minutes later she handed me a mug which said, 'No. 1.'

'Try that.'

She stood over me, watching me try it.

'Phew, bit strong, isn't it?'

'Cures all known hangovers.'

I took another sip. 'I think I'd rather be uncured.'

'Shall I make it weaker?'

'No, no, I'm trying a lot of new things tonight.'

A smile tugged at the corners of her mouth.

'You hated that ciggie Steve gave you, didn't you?'

'Well, er . . .'

'Tell the truth.'

'I hated it.'

She laughed delightedly.

'I knew it. I was watching your expression. I hated smoking for ages. Two puffs behind the bushes were enough for me. What about the lager?'

'Sort of bitter but after a while you don't notice the

flavour any more – and I really liked sitting there with the drink in my hand. I felt adult and right.'

'I know what you mean. When I was younger – a lot younger – I used to sit upstairs, a glass in my hand, holding conversations with myself. And do you know what I was drinking?'

'No.'

'Vinegar.'

'What!'

'Yes, I'd fill one of Mum's glasses with vinegar and sit up there, sipping away, thinking I was it.' She chuckled to herself as she settled herself on the camp bed, even pillowing her head as if she was getting ready to sleep.

'When I was nine I drank a whole bottle of Martini,' she continued. 'I was sick for days. I get really bored of drinking now.' There was a pause.

'You do a lot of drawing,' I remarked conversationally.

'Yeah, I love drawing. Not what we do at school, but designing things.'

'What sort of things?'

'Costume jewellery, that sort of thing.'

I started looking through a pad. 'Those are really good.'

'No, no, they're rubbish. Look at the next pad – the one with the nude woman in front – that's Steve's.'

'Oh.' The name I'd deliberately avoided mentioning all evening had suddenly been spoken.

'Yeah. He's pretty good actually, does sort of cartoon sketches. He did some of me, really funny ones.'

'He came round here a lot then?' I asked, my curiosity

overcoming my feeling that this wasn't really any of my business.

'All the time. Before we went out together we got on really well. I think he saw me as a mate. Then one day he came round and asked me out – all of a sudden.'

'And you accepted?'

'Has anyone ever refused Steve?'

'How long did it last?'

'Forty-seven days. Then the night before my party he came in here, put his arms round me and hugged me really tightly. That's when I knew something was wrong, because normally he'd just fling himself on the camp bed and say, "Make us a coffee, Ash," or something.'

I snuggled down, feeling remarkably relaxed while Ashley went on, 'Then Steve said how great I was, how we'd always be good friends, really good friends – but the time was right for a change.'

'What did you say?'

'One word: Anna. I knew he'd been after her, every bloke had, for years. But she only went out with "safe" blokes who were about twenty, and specially approved by her parents. Steve was the first guy from our school to be honoured.'

'You don't like Anna?'

'Most of the time she's my best friend.'

'Really?' I was astonished.

'It's funny, we've been friends for years and never fought over a bloke. Always gone our own way – before Steve. It would be Steve we both want, wouldn't it?' A bitterness entered her voice. 'Not that I think Anna loves Steve or anything, she just loves having her own way. Whatever Anna wants she gets. And at the moment it's Steve. But he's just a novelty. They're not suited.'

'They're not? They seemed pretty suited tonight.'

'No, Anna likes her blokes under the thumb. Steve won't take that. I give it two or three weeks – at the most,' her confident tone splintered away. 'And then one day I'll come in here, I'll see this pair of boots by the door. Did you know Steve always puts his change in his boots before he lies down?' She laughed fondly. 'And there he'll be, sprawled out on a camp bed, that daft smile on his face as he says, "Make us a coffee, Ash." And he'll act as if he's never been away. He won't apologise or anything. Steve could never do that. But I'll smile back at him and throw his sketch pads back at him and I'll say, "See – I kept them all – I knew you'd come back to me".'

I sat up, scanning Ashley's face. Her eyes were closed. But I knew, behind her eyes it was all coming true and she was living every moment of it. When you've been getting your fix out of day-dreaming as long as me you can easily recognise a fellow-sufferer.

And all of a sudden, I could feel high volts of sympathy passing between us. Every time I thought of her a great current of affection surged through me. These currents were pretty high-powered too, wiping out all my concerns. All I could think about now was Ashley. And as she spoke, I seemed to be not just listening, but absorbing her every word.

'You know, Ricky, tonight when Steve was so distant and strange to me, I was very upset – at first. But then I thought, perhaps he's being like that because he doesn't trust himself with me. Do you think that might be true?'

'Yes, yes,' I said fervently. I was sitting up while Ashley was still lying flat out, eyes tightly closed. Looking down on her like this I felt like her psychiatrist. I gazed affectionately at my patient. 'What you say could well be true,' I declared authoritatively.

'Steve will never admit it, of course. He's such a baby really – a baby – and a pig.'

She said the word 'pig' so affectionately, it sounded like a compliment.

'But Steve and I. We've had so many good times, we always seemed to be laughing and fooling about. And all those good times, they just can't disappear, can they?'

'No,' I said. Ash was staring at me, almost begging me to say something more and I couldn't let her down. From the murky depths of my mind I said, 'Do not grieve, forever wilt thou love and it will never pass into nothingness.'

Instantly, Ash's eyes shot open, they were shining with joy. 'But that's beautiful. I wish I could quote things like that. Where did you read that?'

I didn't like to say it was one of the bits I'd learnt for my Keats essay during the Mocks. So I said mysteriously, 'I don't quite remember,' then added, in a grave 'Now

110

we'll say the Lords Prayer' voice, 'Such love as yours cannot fade or . . .' I was getting muddled now. I quickly concluded '. . . or be denied.' Then I burped and tasted the kipper I'd eaten two days earlier. But Ash was out of her camp bed and in my arms now, all soft and warm and grateful and impressed. 'You're so clever, Ricky. You have so much in that head of yours. I could never quote beautiful poetry like that. And you're so nice, so really nice. I'm very glad we became friends.'

By now, so many currents of affection were leaping through me I expected a fuse to blow any second. Every time Ashley spoke my feelings crackled and popped and there was a strange sensation below my navel too – a sort of wonderful itchiness. Ash went on – 'You know, I'll never forget the day of that awful bus crash. I was so shocked when everyone said you'd been killed. And then when I was in the middle of collecting money for you – and you appeared before me. You know, it was like a miracle. For at twelve o'clock you were dead and at one o'clock – alive.' She said that last word so softly and caressingly.

'Yet, in a funny awful sort of way, that bus crash did us a good turn. I mean, for years I'd known you and not known you. I'd see you in the front of the class, scribbling away, comparing marks with Mouse, but I just thought, there's a boffin, that's all. And if that bus accident hadn't happened and made me notice you I'd never have realised you were like this. You're so different to how I imagined.'

'I am?'

'Oh yes, you're so sympathetic and . . .'

She gasped in amazement. So did I as the shed was suddenly plunged into darkness.

She shot up. 'The lights can't have gone off. Not all of them,' she cried.

'Probably fused,' I said, feeling very fused myself.

But then we heard a faint but unmistakable tapping noise – four slow, steady taps on the window.

'What's that?' I cried.

'I don't know,' said Ashley, 'but let's get out of here.'

I jumped out of the camp bed so quickly, it snapped back on me.

'Are you all right?' hissed Ashley. For some reason we were whispering.

'I'm okay, but the camp bed . . .'

'Never mind that. Come on, Ricky.'

'Keep talking then,' I said. My eyes hadn't yet got used to the dark. As I stumbled forward four more taps could be heard. Someone or something wanted to come in.

'Who's there?' called Ashley bravely.

I muttered too, just to show Ash I was backing her up. No answer. Then just as we reached the door, a new sound. The sound of someone impersonating a ghost – badly. 'Aaaaarrrr' it went, then 'Be – w – a r e, Be – w – a r e.'

'Someone's idea of a joke,' muttered Ashley, 'and I think I know who.'

'Not Steve?'

'No, he's miles away and besides, it's too amateurish for him. But I know who it is.'

Ashley flung open the door. I was right behind her, gaping at a small man in a striped jacket.

'Oh Dad, it was funny the first time.'

'It's funny every time.'

He had a bright baby face and a bright foolish smile. Only the rings round his neck hinted at his age.

He gave me the once-over. 'This is a new one.'

'Dad, meet Ricky. I told you about him. He's the boy who was in that bus crash in . . .'

'Oh yes, bad business that. Well, you are very welcome, young man, but time is marching on and even my daughter needs her beauty sleep, you know.' He was trying to be jolly but I didn't feel he really was jolly.

'Ash, would you like a coffee?' a voice called.

A very pretty woman was standing by the back door. I liked her instantly.

'It's all right, we've had coffee,' said Ash.

The woman made a mock grimace. 'Oh dear, well don't let that put . . .'

'Ricky,' prompted Ash.

'Don't be put off, Ricky, I make proper coffee.'

'Denise, I'm just trying to pack this pair off to bed,' said Ashley's dad.

'Yes, it's all right, I'm off,' I said.

'You don't smell too bad to me,' he said, grinning away.

'Oh Dad, go in, it's far too late for your jokes. I won't be long,' said Ash.

He patted me on the back. 'Nice seeing you.' He paused. I knew he'd forgotten my name already. 'You'll have to tell us about your brush with death one day, eh?'

He swaggered towards his wife.

'Goodnight, Ricky,' she called. 'See you again.'

'Yes, goodnight to you,' I said.

The door closed.

'That's my family,' said Ashley, half-apologetically, half-affectionately.

'I like them,' I said. 'Your mum's really nice.'

'Yes, she is – but she's not my mum. She's my dad's live-in girlfriend.'

'Oh,' I said, embarrassed.

'My mum is in London now with my big sister Jo. She walked out on my dad last year. He was carrying on with some Swedish tart then. She was awful, always trying to order me about. But Denise – that's who you just met – she's nice. It's not the same as having my mum here, though.'

'No, of course not,' I said, feeling slightly bewildered by this rush of family news.

'Anyway, I suppose I'd better go in. He's in a good mood now because he's wasted, but his moods change by the second.'

I had no wish to see her dad – or his ever-changing moods – again. So I chanted, almost without thinking, 'Bye then, Ash. I have enjoyed myself. Thank you very much for inviting me round for coffee.'

She gave a tiny swoon. 'But haven't you got lovely manners. Most blokes just slope off after – after coffee. Not so much as a thank you.'

I blushed with pleasure.

'And thank you for listening to me ranting on about Steve. I do stop talking occasionally, you know.'

She gave a rather sad half-laugh. And right then I wanted to switch on her look of joy once more.

So I said, 'And Ash, if I can do anything to help you and Steve,' I noticed a slight quiver about her neck whenever I said his name, 'just ask me.'

'You're sweet,' she whispered.

Then came my punch-line. 'I am certain of nothing but the holiness of the heart's affections.' More English homework. But Ash was drinking in my words – she obviously appreciated the poetry more than me. 'So I have no doubt, no doubt at all, that you and Steve will be back together any day now.' Then I decided to get her really joyous by adding, 'Perhaps even this weekend.'

As I left, Ash's face was so lit up with happiness, I had to keep staring back at her. I'd left her – happy. I'd really helped her. Hadn't I?

Next morning I wasn't so sure. I'd given her hope but was it false hope? Would Steve leave Anna for Ash? Did he really care about Ash? I thought of his crude comments about her down the pub. Was he covering up deeper feelings? I suddenly realised I'd been advising Ash out of total ignorance. But because I'm a boffin and get top marks at school and can learn a few quotes, Ash is hanging on my every word. And right now I've got her all set for a happy ending. But what if . . . What have I done?

A Mighty Gut and a Stray Tongue

Right from the start Sunday was weird. Well, from breakfast anyway. That was when Mum sat opposite me, looking grave. I braced myself for a talk on crusts.

For this weekend I finally succumbed to the slimming bug. Mum might claim my barrels of excess weight are due to hormonal imbalance – not over-eating – but I've decided to help my hormones out. So for breakfast I'm only eating bacon, eggs, fried bread, two rounds of toast – and I'm leaving every single one of my crusts. Actually, I've always left my crusts but now I'm doing so determinedly.

I prepare for battle. But to my amazement crusts are ignored. She must have an even weightier matter on her mind. She says, 'Wear your nice new shirt this afternoon, Nip – the one I bought you. Your sister will like that.'

I nod reluctantly.

Mum adds matter-of-factly, 'And I've left you out fresh boxer shorts.'

'Mum, must we talk about my boxers over breakfast?' I say, pushing the plate containing the unchewed crusts nearer to her, almost willing her to fire the first shot. But instead, she says pacifyingly, 'Now don't be annoyed because I tell you things like that. I'm your best friend if you did but know it.'

I glance at my best friend. Once I told you everything. But now there's already so much I can never tell you. And each day there's going to be more, until a great gulf forms, marking off your world from mine. Blissfully unaware of her fate Mum chatters on – and on . . . 'And your sister's going to be pleased to see you looking so well. She was so worried about you last time, especially when you . . .'

'Mum,' I shoot her a warning glance.

'I know it's a painful subject, Nip. But I blame myself. I should never have let you work so hard for all your exams. Why, you never stepped out of your room except at meal-times. And that wasn't right. And at night when I switched my light off I should have made you switch your light off too. I'm just thankful that awful rash hasn't come back. Kay's always asking me . . .'

I turn away. Trust Mum to bring that up. It was bad enough at the time when I discovered this huge, ugly rash slithering down me, without being reminded about it now. I don't need reminding. Aren't I always checking the scene of its invasion – especially at night? That's when I frighten myself rashes are sprouting all over again.

'Nip, that rash was Nature's way of telling you to slow down. As Dr Jameson said, its cause was psychological.'

117

'A prime case of mind over matter,' I interrupt wearily. 'Dr Jameson said that half the people in hospital are sick not because of their body – but their mind.'

'Exactly,' Mum claps her hands together excitedly, the way they do on quiz shows when you answer the star question correctly.

'I knew you'd understand,' then leaning forward she says in one of her whispers which are more piercing than her normal voice, 'So this afternoon when Kay and her husband arrive for their very nice visit, I know you won't be alarmed by any changes.'

'Changes?'

Mum becomes flustered. 'Bodily changes caused by – well, er – when one is pregnant certain changes, certain bodily changes occur . . .'

I don't believe it. Mum is giving me a sex education lesson. The kind you give a backward five-year-old. So with heavy sarcasm I interrupt.

'Mum, you're not telling me that babies aren't found under gooseberry bushes, are you? I must say I thought it was strange, never finding one there as I've often looked but I assumed they arrived with the morning dew.'

'All right son. I only wanted to prepare you for what you might see . . .' Her assumption that I know nothing so infuriates me. I'm shrieking, 'Mum, I do know about pregnancies and babies and wombs and S – E – X.'

She springs to her feet.

'Right, fine, that will do, thank you very much.'

She frantically scoops up the dirty plates.

'I'm not staying here to have you shouting the odds at me. I don't deserve that.'

She inserts a pause which I'm supposed to fill with apologies. I say nothing. But Mum simply adds, as if I had apologised, 'I know you didn't mean to shout and the subject is a delicate one and perhaps not suitable for the breakfast table.' She takes up her pacifying tone again, 'And anyway, you're a very sensible young man and I'm sure you will be understanding. I just wanted to warn you . . .'

'Warn me?' I splutter. Before I can say any more Mum swirls the plates in front of her as if she's a matador warding off a mad bull.

'Not another word,' she roars. 'Not one. The subject is closed.'

Mum leaves me, fuming.

What a performance and over what? The fact that my sister is heavy with child and Mum thinks I won't know what's happening to her. I pace angrily around the room. After the glitter and excitement of Friday I'm back to Mum saying – 'Change your boxers, and don't be frightened of your sister's big tum'. How can I bear another day confined here? Saturday had been deadly enough but Sunday is going to creak by. Upstairs I hear Mum murmuring away to Dad. He'll be lying in bed, covered in the Sunday papers. I hear his very low rumble. Why are they both whispering? And why is everything here so drab and stale and dull and shrunken?

Overnight, I've out-grown this house. I don't belong

here any more. For one mad moment I want to fling myself against the glass and break out of this aquarium before I'm stifled to death.

Oh where are Steve, Ashley and the gang? That's where I belong, where there's colour and energy and people who aren't afraid to shout or laugh. Yesterday, I'd even hoped one of the gang would ring me up. For on Friday hadn't I passed all the tests and given Ashley good advice? Advice anyhow.

Mum comes back downstairs, plonking her head round the door. She's switched into her normal tone. 'Your father was gasping for his second cup. I'll do my nets now. Don't forget, clean boxers and socks, all waiting for you in the airing cupboard. And if you could give your bedroom a tidy up and a quick dust, just in case Kay goes upstairs, we want it nice and tidy for her, don't we?'

I could hardly stop myself from yawning. And why all this high-powered preparation? Anyone would think Kay had never lived here. But she had. Once. She'd been my sister then. And she'd had beautiful blonde hair, a figure any beauty queen would have envied and a fun personality anyone would have envied. She was as popular as I was unpopular. While I languished in the second year, she ruled the fifth year. Bit like Anna, really.

Of course, we had cargoes of boyfriends round here; that was fun too. For after the latest one had gone she'd sit on my bed (I was, of course, always at my desk swotting) and tell me how awful he was and make me laugh and feel great. Until one day Justin came round.

And afterwards I waited for her to tell me how awful he was. But instead, she was ages outside, seeing him off. And I watched her out of Mum's window, sniggering and whispering and behaving really childishly with him. And when he finally left she just called 'Goodnight' to me and ran into her bedroom.

Soon he was round here all the time. And he was awful, really phoney and pretentious – the sort of guy who can't say 'shop' but has to say 'retail outlet'. And when Mum asked him if he wanted a cup of tea, he'd give one of his awful smiles which showed all his gums and say in a really cringy way, 'All right then, why not? You've persuaded me'. And he was very tall and skinny and had these high white collars which he was always fiddling with, reminding me of a preening giraffe.

He made my flesh crawl, but my sister was mad on him. And I always knew when she'd seen him, for every time he kissed her she became a little uglier. By the time she married him my sister had lost all her looks – and me.

So when, at two o'clock, Mum did her breathless 'They're here' bit, I followed my parents coolly and at a distance. I was greeting a distant descendant of someone I'd once loved – that's all.

Mum gave Kay her embarrassing bearhug welcome. Dad gave Kay his even more embarrassing 'I'm too choked up to speak' welcome, while Kay and I exchanged tiny, dead kisses.

'Your hair!' she cried.

'Took the garden shears to it,' joked Dad.

'And it's nothing to do with me,' said Mum quickly.

Actually, Kay didn't look as bad as I'd feared. All those whispered phone-calls she and Mum kept having had worried me – a little. But Kay was only slightly uglier than the last time I'd seen her. She did have some brown blotches on her face which looked like coffee stains but probably weren't – while her belly swelled most impressively. I thought of the life locked inside that womb and sympathised with it. But just before husband Justin came into view, Mum actually stepped in front of me whispering, 'Steady, steady'.

Later I was to be grateful to her for doing that – and rather guilty too. For it was not the sight of Kay Mum had been trying to prepare me for at breakfast but the sight of . . .

When I tell you about Justin now, you'll laugh. Why not? Feel free. Only it wasn't funny then. Not completely. It was grotesque, sick, spooky – and funny. I wanted to stare and stare at him, crack up and – shrink away in horror. Instead, Justin and I shook hands and he had a faint, rather sinister smile on his face, while I knew I had a look of shock and horror on mine. How else can you look when you come face to face with a guy that looks as if he's downed forty pints in one go? I tell you, he had a gut on him the like of which I'd never seen before. And I doubt if you have.

Or perhaps you have. It happens from time to time apparently. The husband becomes so involved with his wife's pregnancy, he starts displaying the same symptoms. Now I knew why Mum had been going on about me and my rash. Swelling stomachs and rashes can both grow out of the mind.

He lumbered into the lounge, small careful steps, balancing himself by walking on his toes – and his weight needed some balancing. Then he and Kay sat on the couch, backs identically straight, lumps to the front. Mum was clearly flustered by this copy-cat pregnancy and started frantically offering food.

'We'd love to, Mother,' said Justin 'but we've only just eaten ourselves.'

'Quite understand,' said Mum, 'you've got to give your stomach a chance to get itself organised again. Let it go down. The food go down, that is.' Covered in embarrassment she said pleadingly, 'Tea anyone?'

'No, you sit down, Mum,' said Kay, 'I know you, on your feet all the time. We haven't come here to make you work.'

I laughed to myself.

'But I do want to tell you about something wonderful that happened on Friday,' said Kay.

'Are you sure you won't have . . .' began Mum.

But Kay was determined to tell us something 'wonderful'.

'Yesterday, just after eleven, I felt my little visitor kicking,' she tapped her lump.

'Ah, bless his little heart,' said Mum.

'But that's not all,' continued Kay. 'For right then

Justin rang me from work and said, "Kay, I've just felt the little blighter kick me," so he experienced the feeling at exactly the same time as me. Isn't that remarkable?'

I thought it was distinctly pervy. And I bet they think he's a right nutcase at work. How could he let that happen to him? Yet, much as I despised him, I couldn't help be a bit fascinated by his phantom pregnancy too. I mean, when would he stop swelling? The second Kay gave birth? And would his stomach just burst open? Could be very messy.

Dad was trying to change the subject, Mum was straining at the leash to make some tea, while Kay wittered on.

'Whenever I see Justin I feel really loved and special. There aren't many husbands who love their wife so much they want to share their pregnancy, are there?'

'You never said if you had a good journey,' Dad replied, while I nearly threw up. My once wonderful sister is lost forever, inside this soppy fatty. What's made her change so completely? She'd say – with a silly flutter, 'It must be Love'. To be honest, I've never quite cracked this love business. But I have sussed that Love = Weird. Look at Justin. Difficult not to look at his mighty gut. It loomed over the room, loomed over me like some strange alien growth from another world.

All of a sudden, Mum switched the conversation from how she knows that Kay's going to have a boy because she looks angular (she didn't predict what Justin was going to have) to me. She goes, 'And our Nip is courting strong, you know.'

'No, not really!' Kay seemed quite shocked.

'That explains the foreign haircut then,' said Justin smugly.

'He took his young lady out for a meal on Friday,' continued Mum coyly.

'I hope you paid,' said Mighty Gut.

I didn't answer.

'We haven't been allowed to meet her yet,' continued Mum, 'but she sounds very nice. Ashley – her name is – Ashley Saltmarsh.'

'Not Jo Saltmarsh's sister?' exclaimed Kay.

'That's right,' I said.

'Well, fancy that. I mean, Jo Saltmarsh was a right . . .' Kay, noticing Mum's expectant face, swallowed what she was about to say. 'Jo Saltmarsh – was a great favourite with the boys, most popular. And so my little brother is going out with her sister.'

'Yes,' I said to a chorus of 'Ooohs'.

I don't know why I lied. Perhaps it was the way Kay said 'my little brother'. Perhaps I wanted to impress everyone. Perhaps I'm just a liar.

Kay was certainly impressed.

'New hairstyle, new girlfriend – I can't keep up with my baby brother.'

'There's something else,' said Mum, 'something I didn't want to worry you about before, when you were so worried about, things.' She half-pointed at Justin's gut. I sensed she was about to tell Kay about the bus crash. But she was interrupted by the doorbell.

'Now, who can that be?' said Mum. 'It can't be the egg-woman for I told her . . .'

'I'll get it,' said Dad, moving surprisingly quickly.

I think Dad found Justin's state highly embarrassing.

Dad returned, looking almost excited.

'It's for you, Richard.'

I started. 'For me?'

'And it's your young lady.'

'Ashley?'

'Of course, how many young ladies have you got?'

I felt embarrassed – and awkward. I didn't want Ashley to see me like this. I didn't have any of Steve's gear on. Instead I was wearing Mum's ghastly 'executive' shirt.

I walked out with my arms folded over my chest. I couldn't subject Ashley to a full frontal of this shirt, not right away.

'Here he is, then,' said Dad.

Embarrassed hellos in the hallway followed.

'I'm awfully sorry to bother you,' said Ashley 'but I accidentally spilt some coke on my geography notes. All the writing started to run and I tried to clear it up but only made it worse – so could I borrow your notes?'

'Yeah, sure.'

Was this really why Ashley had come round? I stared at Dad, wishing he'd exit but he was doing his conversational stuff.

'Geography notes, eh?' he said.

'That's right.'

'Ah, smudged your geography notes, eh? Can't have

that.' he laughed and so did we. 'Smudged geography notes, eh?'

We laughed again. Dad was about to meditate further on the subject when a voice called – 'Don't leave Ashley standing in the hallway, show her into the dining room.'

Dad obediently became doorman, while Mum hovered.

'I'm sure Ashley would like a nice cup of tea, wouldn't you?' Mum said.

'If it's no trouble.'

'I'll do it, Mum.'

'No you won't. When you pour a cup of tea out you leave a pound of sugar on the tray. I make a good cup of tea, even if I say so myself. Milk and sugar, Ashley dear?'

'Please.'

'I expect you wouldn't say "No" to one of my coconut cakes, either.'

Mum left Ashley sitting by the window and me crouching in the darkest part of the room. If only I wasn't wearing this shirt. I decided to offer an explanation straightaway.

'Sorry about the shirt. I've been decorating. And whenever I decorate I always wear this really old, ghastly shirt.'

I stared down at the shirt, gleaming its awful newness.

'It's a funny old shirt. Years old and still looks like new.'

'That's handy,' said Ashley and she looked at me quite affectionately I thought. Suddenly I noticed – 'Your hair, it's changed to jet black.'

'I wondered when you'd realise.'

'I like it. But what made you change?'

'Oh, I got bored of it. Anyhow, it went all luminous in the sun.'

'It did? What sun?'

'The sun from my sun lamp,' she smiled. 'And by the way, Ricky, don't go looking for your geography book.' And as she said that she flashed me this cheeky grin.

That grin managed to crack open the frozen wastes below my navel. I was experiencing the first stages of being turned on – in Mum's dining room, too.

'No, it isn't your geography book I want,' Ashley said, smiling again.

'So what do you want? My body?'

Immediately after I said that I started laughing – so Ashley would think I was joking.

'Perhaps later,' she said, 'but first I've come to beg a favour.'

'Beg away.'

She squirmed. 'Oh, I really hate asking you this – and Ricky – if you think this is a cheek you will say so, won't you?'

'Yeah, sure.'

I was distinctly intrigued now.

'Okay, here goes. On Friday night you helped me a great deal.'

'Oh no, all I did . . .'

'Yes, you did. Do you know, you're the only person I can trust. I mean, anyone else I'd told about Steve and me would have blabbed it all round Wycombe by now. And

Ricky, what you said about Steve and me getting back together very soon, well, I kept thinking about that.'

I hoped I wasn't blushing.

'But then, last night I got a bit silly, went all upset again. I started playing these records and it seemed as if every song was about me and Steve. It's crazy but do you know what I mean?'

I didn't quite, but I nodded anyhow.

'And then last night, Ricky, I had the weirdest dream. Would you believe I was having my portrait painted? That's a laugh, isn't it? But the weird thing was I couldn't see who was painting me. All I could see were these hands – and I could see them really clearly – they must have been lit up or something. They were very large hands with long, strong fingers.'

I cast a glance downwards. No, definitely not mine.

'Then, just as I was stretching forward to see who the hands belonged to, I woke up. I was so disappointed until I realised whose hands they were – they could only be Steve's hands.'

'Ah,' I said, thinking some response was expected.

'And do you know, Ricky, I think that dream was a sign. It was saying to me, Stop waiting for Steve to make the first move – for he's so proud he might never do it. But what about if I make it easier for Steve and go round to him?' She looked at me expectantly, hopefully. 'Do you understand?' she asked softly.

I couldn't understand at all how a dream about hands – which might be Steve's – meant she should go round his house. But I felt she was relying on me to agree with her. So I said, 'Yes, I understand, perfectly.'

'I knew you would,' she leaned forward. 'Now, Ricky, here's the favour. I don't want to go round when my former best friend's there.'

'Anna?'

'Yes, so I was wondering would you mind ringing up Steve, checking she's not with him – and perhaps putting in a good word for old Ash? Would you mind?'

'If you think it would help.'

'Oh yes. Definitely. Steve respects your intelligence. He told me that.'

That pleased me. 'Okay, Ash, of course I will.'

She stood up. 'Come here.'

I trotted towards her like some obedient puppy, totally unprepared for what happened next.

Of course I've been hugged before. Scores of times, if you count an eighty-three-year-old great-aunt. But there's a world of difference between a great aunt's hug – even one trying her best – and an Ashley hug.

Ashley's hug is much tighter with even our cheeks touching and much hotter and it makes my eyes tickle and itch. By the time it ends I'm stuck with all these tears getting ready to drop. It's the shock that causes them, of course, that and the fact that Ashley's hug is the best thing that's ever happened to me. And I pretend to be clearing the table for our tea so Ashley won't notice I've become a bit water-logged and my glasses need windscreen wipers. But then she comes over to me and I think she has noticed and I'm about to say something corny to her – the kind of thing they're always saying in adverts – but instead she just says, 'Would you mind ringing Steve now?'

In a total daze I dialled Steve's number. (Of course she knows it by heart. Probably says it in her sleep.)

I was about to put the phone down again when I heard a voice say, 'Hello, Chinese Laundry'. What stopped me was some muffled laughing in the background.

'Who is this?' I asked.

'This is honourable "Suck Fou" – more laughing.

I think I recognised Danny's laugh.

'Fou y-o-u?' said the voice.

'Rick – ou,' I replied.

A pause, then in Steve's normal voice, 'Ricky, my main man, how's it going?'

'Fine.'

'I meant to give you a buzz yesterday but Danny dragged me to this wedding which turned into one almighty drinking session.'

'He got paralytic,' called Danny.

'At least I didn't try and get off with that rough old tart . . .' scuffling noises followed before Steve returned, shouting, 'Danny's bit was gross – and I mean gross.'

Danny said something I couldn't hear and then Steve said, 'How did Friday up Ash go? And Danny says was there any rumpy pumpy – 'cause he hasn't had it for so long he gets his cheapies hearing about other people's action.'

'Actually, Ash is here now,' I said.

I hoped Ash couldn't hear all the whistles and chantings of 'Drop 'em' which followed that news.

Then there was some more scuffling before an alien voice said, 'Get in there, mate.' 'That was my brother Andy,' said Steve. 'He's an ugly git. All right, you can clear off now, Andy. Go and make us some more dinner.'

Danny called, 'Andy's food tastes like the kind of thing you avoid treading on, it's . . .' Then it sounded as if Danny had been whacked on the head.

I stared across at Ashley – all tense and hopeful – but there was no way I could have a serious conversation about her now – so instead when Steve returned I asked, 'What are you doing tonight?'

'Taking the missus out.'

'Taking your mum out?' I was amazed.

'No, Anna, you plonker.'

'Oh, of course.'

'We're going to Tiffany's again. Danny's too much of a girly to go.'

'Got to get some pence in my pocket,' wailed Danny.

'Pick you up if you want,' said Steve, 'be full of girls, just asking for it.'

'Another time,' I said.

I couldn't leave Ashley now. 'Bit tired today.'

Steve laughed. 'That's Ash for you.'

I felt a spurt of jealousy. How many blokes has Ashley gone with?

Steve's tone became more serious. 'Don't get too hung up on Ash, though. She's all right – but if you're not careful she'll never let you alone.'

'Oh really?' That sounded quite good to me. By the time Steve rang off I'd convinced myself that he didn't care for Ash. It was Anna he wanted. He even called Anna 'the missus'. Ash was too heavy for Steve and he obviously didn't understand her. But I did. I did!

I said to Ash, 'Sorry I couldn't say much, Danny was there and Steve's brother.'

'Which one?'

'Andy.'

'He's a slob, they're all slobs – except Steve.'

'Steve's out with Anna tonight too.'

'Mmm.'

'Going to Tiffany's again.'

'How boring.'

I paused.

'And Ash . . .' I stared at her, so intoxicated, I dared to . . . 'Ash, stand up a minute.'

She stood up.

And then for one of the few times in my life I acted completely on impulse. I dived my lips at Ash's, then plunged my tongue through her mouth, as I'd seen Anna and Steve do on Friday. Then I waited for the frenching and the squishing noises. But instead, my tongue just fluttered up and down Ash's mouth, like a trapped butterfly. And I knew from Ash's gasp of horror when I'd inserted my tongue – and the way she felt all tense and stiff and resistant – that I'd performed yet another belly-flop.

I released her mouth from my tongue and shrugged my shoulders apologetically, as if my tongue had jumped its lead without me realising it. And I said, 'Sorry if I surprised you but Steve said to give you a surprise kiss.'

Her look of bewilderment instantly evaporated.

'Oh how sweet of him.'

And a new expression crossed her face – but I couldn't look at her any more. I was tired of borrowing Steve's things.

And when Ashley left, full of thanks and Mum's tea, I still couldn't look at her properly. I'd spent the time exaggerating, if not creating, Steve's feelings for Ashley to cover up . . .

If only I hadn't done it, I could have spent the rest of the evening dreaming about Ashley's hug, imagining one molecule of her fancied me. But now I knew the truth. Her hug was just a firmer, juicier version of the kind eighty-three-year-old great-aunts give out. And certainly not the kind of hug designed to encourage anything. I shuddered. I don't think I'll ever forget Ashley's gasps of shock when my tongue paid her a call. I can only compare her gasps to those emitted by people unfortunate enough to have buckets of freezing cold water thrown over them.

My sister left soon after Ashley. Once, I think I could have told her about my feeble frenching. I wanted to, now.

But my sister and I hadn't spoken properly today, and it was highly unlikely we ever would again. Yet, when she kissed me goodbye, she whispered, 'Look out for yourself now,' and I whispered back, 'And you look after yourself,' and we both meant it. Funny how difficult it is to stop caring about people – even when you've nothing in common with them any more.

When Justin heaved himself into the driving seat he and Kay looked such a sight, like something out of a comic horror film, I burst out laughing – to my mum's disgust. After which I rushed upstairs to my bedroom to do something very dangerous.

Yesterday, I'd smuggled my Friday-night clothes – my real clothes – into the bottom of my school bag. They were there now. And although it was perilous and foolhardy, Mum could barge in at any minute, I put them all on again. I had to check, just in case there was the faintest chance . . .

I squared up to the mirror, faced it longer than I'd ever dared before and came to one conclusion – even in Steve's clothes – I have all the sex appeal of a dead halibut. The 'me' in the mirror: glasses, fat, zitty, ugly – no amount of clothes can camouflage that 'me'. As the Chinese proverb says, 'You can't paint a beautiful picture on the shell of a rotten egg.'

How could I blame Ashley for gasping when I kissed her? No girl could fancy me, unless she was wearing a blindfold. But girls, this ugly frame of a body is an imposter, it isn't the real me. Can't any girl see that?

I try to cheer up by telling myself jokes about my appearance. I'm so funny I end up sprawled on the floor, sobbing my guts out. Until finally, I'm all cried out, all feeling wrung out of me. And I start giving myself these little pep talks.

I've got to forget girls – even Ashley – as there's obviously nothing doing there. Best to concentrate on what I can achieve. Aren't I already shaking off my boffin stigma, even becoming a bit popular? And if I keep on – why, I could be up there with the Lads.

By next morning the pep talk has taken effect and I spring out of bed. I've got it all worked out. Now I know what I must do.

One Month Later – The Real Me!

Richard Hodgson
25 January

LIFE SKILLS : CLASSWORK : YOU HAVE RETURNED
FROM A HOLIDAY AND JUST DISCOVERED THAT YOU
LEFT BEHIND A VALUABLE ARTICLE. WRITE A
LETTER TO THE MANAGER EXPLAINING FULLY WHAT
YOU THINK HAS HAPPENED.

I Cretin Crescent,

Dear Commandant
On returning home from your prison-camp style, derelict
hotel, very fittingly situated between Greasy Joe's Chip Take-
away and Big Brenda's Massage Parlour, I noticed something
missing.

My excessively expensive gold watch with diamond-studded

gold bracelet and free one-year no-quibble money-back guar-antee was gone.

That chalet maid nicked it. I thought she took a long time making the bed. I'm not sure of her name but she's got shifty eyes and a dead suspicious grin.

So will you please string her up immediately and send me snapshots. Alternatively, let a hundred dogs savage her.
Yours

I'd been dreading this.

As I approached her she was deep in thought, re-flecting on me, I guessed. She was also absent-mindedly fanning herself with a card. My card. My report card.

'Please sit down, Richard.' Even when she was about to give you a rollicking Ma Divvy was polite and pleasant. That's why I dreaded being told off by her. I didn't quite trust myself with such a decent teacher.

'Miss, can't you just give me the report card? I'm starv-ing for my lunch?'

'No, I can't.' She remained polite but firm, adding, 'I want to understand. I want to help you.'

I sat down, sighing loudly. All my life I'd heard pupils sighing like that. Now I was doing it, expertly!

But Ma Divvy was too good a teacher to acknow-ledge my performance. Instead she looked straight at me then, after a brief unnerving silence, asked 'What's happening?'

'Nothing.' I slouched down my chair, just as Steve had taught me.

'No, Richard, for some weeks things have been going badly wrong – ever since your bus crash . . .'

She waited for me to respond. I just peered over the top of her blonde helmet of hair. She leaned forward, straining to make contact. 'Richard, I do know a little of the effects of – an accident. Only recently I went out for a what I imagined was a quiet Sunday afternoon drive when just as I – and the car in front of me – were slowing down to turn right, this MG came speeding behind me. It couldn't slow down in time and it went right into me, pushing me into the car in front . . .' She gave a nervous laugh. 'You could say I was the jam in the sandwich.'

'Were you hurt?'

'The whiplash injury jolted my neck and that was pretty painful – but I was lucky, really. But you know, Richard – when I stepped out of my car and saw all these cars wrecked and this young couple weeping in each other's arms and so many other things . . . I knew I'd never be able to totally forget them. They'd left their mark on me. For days afterwards I'd wake up, feeling all unhinged and strange. My world had received a nasty jolt – just like yours did recently.'

I lowered my head. This wasn't playing fair. How dare she be so human.

'And Richard, it might be a cliché but you must hold on to the thought that even after a ghastly accident – Life does go on. It really does. And your life is so full of promise. Already you've achieved so much.'

'Oh really?' I said bitterly. 'Passing a few exams, you

mean.' I stopped. It was dangerous to explain myself to the enemy. And she was the enemy. As Steve said, 'When it comes to it, teachers all stick together.'

'You are a brilliant pupil, Richard,' she continued, 'and you should gain excellent results this summer. You deserve those results. Only don't let yourself be cheated of them by certain members of your form who are leading you astray.'

I didn't respond. I'd already said too much. I examined the floor closely as she said, 'Your escaping a bus crash has given you a certain – a certain glamour to your form. They've shown an interest in you, but you've let them take you over.'

'That's rubbish,' I whispered.

'Is it? I don't think so. Last week, for example, you had a group detention for not doing the English homework – but then when I look in your English book I find it's there all along. You know what I think? You were scared to admit you'd done a homework. That's it, isn't it?'

'I just forgot I'd done it, that's all!' I was still deeply ashamed of my lapse.

'And interestingly, I receive more complaints about your behaviour in Social Education and Art – the two subjects you share with Steve Almond and Danny Stapleton – than any other. Just this break-time Mr Kendal stopped me and said he had to send you out of the Art block today – is that right?'

'If he says so.'

'What did he send you out for?'

I squirmed. This was becoming embarrassing.

'He sent me out for laughing.'

'Laughing?'

'Laughing,' I echoed flatly. 'He came into the room saying "All right, lads, get your tools out," and everyone thought that was pretty funny, but only I got shouted at.'

Ma Divvy shook her head. 'And Miss Punchin says you mess around in her class just to show off to Steve and Danny. She showed me the letter you wrote for Life Skills.

'What did you think?'

'If you'd written it for me I'd say mildly funny – but in Miss Punchin's case I'd say cruel. You know she's a new teacher still settling in and she can't cope with that sort of thing yet. But you let Steve and Danny egg you on.'

'No, not at all.'

'So why do you misbehave in Miss Punchin's class then?'

I gave an answer I'd often heard Steve give.

'Because she's boring.' I added, 'Also she wears cowboy boots. And she's got this baby doll on top of her desk and she's always standing by this doll and smiling at it. I think she's . . .'

'Stop this nonsense!' Ma Divvy's face tightened up. It was the closest she came to shouting.

'This is not you I'm listening to. This is Steve Almond.'

'Not, it's not! It's me. The real me. Steve helped me find a voice – but this is me talking.'

'No, it's not.'

'Yes, it is. I should know, shouldn't I?'

Her voice almost broke with anguish. 'Oh, please stop this charade, Richard. You're throwing away a lifetime's work for one fleeting moment of popularity. I know you had a bad experience recently and I've bent over backwards to make allowances for . . . what are you laughing at?'

'I was just thinking of you bending over backwards. It must be pretty difficult. Can you bend right back?'

I watched her face freeze up. At last I was having an effect. Now she was all wound up, far more upset with me that she would have been with Steve or Danny. It's always worse when your pet poodle suddenly bites your hand.

I kept up my bright, Steve-like tone as she hated that so much.

'All right if I shuffle off now?'

She released a great whopper of a sigh. Then in a formal 'I'm reading you your rights' voice said, 'Your report card must be handed to your teacher at the beginning of every lesson. At the end of the lesson you collect the card which will be signed by your teacher – a comment about your behaviour may be added. At 3.45 p.m. sharp, you bring the card to me. If I am busy you wait. You must not leave school before I have seen your card. And if I am not satisfied with the comments I will send you and your card to the Headmaster.' Then suddenly, pleadingly, 'And you don't want to see the Headmaster, do you?'

'Wouldn't mind, just to see what he looks like . . .'

'Oh Richard, Richard, don't let yourself be pushed down this slippery slope. Please!'

I stood up loudly and noisily. I had to get away from her, double-quick. 'See you then,' I said. 'Cheers for the card.'

A defeated hand waved me away. But just as I was leaving she piped up, 'If ever you do want to talk, I'm always here.'

'At the moment, all I want is my lunch.' I left her, gazing after me in grieving bewilderment.

I shot towards my locker, a little shaken but victorious. I've shown Ma Divvy that I've changed sides. And if I can stand up to her – my favourite teacher – I can stand up to them all. Steve will be proud of me. But before I see Steve I must change my shoes.

Whenever teachers see me they order me to take off my trainers and plonk on regulation footwear. But as soon as they're out of eyeshot, it's on with the trainers again.

As I bend down I wince with pain.

Two days after joining Danny at that body-building class I still ached with stiffness. You see, Danny'd decided that as my dieting wasn't having much (to be honest – any) effect I ought to turn my fat into muscle. But the morning after the body-building class I woke up, paralysed. I couldn't move anything at first. Doing up the buttons on my shirt took half an hour. Danny said the stiffness is caused by muscle sores. I'm certainly sore but where are the muscles?

I carefully eased myself up and collided with Mouse. Typical Mouse: walking around the school, head in a book.

I stepped back from him, rubbing my shoulder.

'Sorry,' said Mouse.

'It's all right. I'm a bit stiff anyway.'

We'd hardly spoken for weeks and it seemed rather strange bumping into him now. After an awkward silence I said, 'Do you still read when you're cycling?'

'Certainly. Provided it's a reasonably straight road you can ignore everything.'

'That's dangerous, Mouse.'

'Breathing is dangerous.' A typical Mouse answer.

He juggled with some books under his arm. 'See these? I've just bought them. Knocked him down to 20p each. Gained two Patricia Highsmith's we haven't read. Crammed full of murders apparently.' He thrust the top two books at me.

I sniffed appreciatively. I get a real fix from the full-blooded musty smell old books give off. When Mouse and I went browsing around the second-hand bookshops I could get high on the smells alone. And I used to imagine I was rescuing every book I bought, taking it to a good home – how pathetic is that?

I edged away from the books and said quickly, 'I've just been putting on my trainers again. No teacher's going to tell me what to wear,' adding in Mouse's language, 'or threaten my individuality.'

'Trainers are nothing but a psychological distraction,' chanted Mouse, then paused. As usual he had a cold on the loose. I watched him flick his head back, sniff deeply and start vacuuming up this stray cold – I'd seen this little ceremony so many times I could watch it almost affectionately now.

Then Mouse half-smiled at me. For him this was being really friendly. Perhaps he had missed me – a tiny bit.

'Haven't seen you much lately?' he said.

'No, been really busy. What with my sister having this baby boy.'

'Seen it yet?'

'Briefly, looks really old. It's got wrinkles, and a really pinched face and no hair. Totally bald.'

Mouse reflected on this. 'Funny to think of babies being born old – and then growing younger every day. Bit like someone I know.'

I got his point.

With elaborate casualness he asked, 'So when are you going to get tired of changing your footwear six times an hour – and only using words of one syllable?'

I smiled. 'Say what you like, Mouse, but you're missing out on so much.'

He shook his head.

'Oh yes you are. Like tonight I'm going out with my mates, meeting some girls, generally having a good time. And what will you be doing, Mouse? Let me guess. Watching a good documentary on rain forests or learning how to make a computer out of two egg cartons . . .'

I stopped sneering. Mouse wasn't interrupting me with one of his cutting retorts – he was just standing there, his shoulders dropping, his whole body wilting before my eyes.

I'd never expected Mouse to be affected by what I said. Not Mouse.

I immediately changed the subject. 'Anyway, you should thank me, Mouse. Aren't you top of the class in everything now?'

Mouse shuffled his books around as if they were cards and mumbled, 'I was quite content being second – to you.' Then he turned away from me. I'd upset him. I really hadn't meant to. I was just . . . just shadow-boxing with him.

Mouse loped off while I ran towards the dinner queue, still in a bit of a daze. I really hadn't meant to get Mouse like that. I like him really.

By the time I reached the queue it was stretching right down the dining hall. Things were obviously moving at a snail's pace today.

I settled myself for a long wait when . . .

'Hey, what's your game?'

It was Steve. 'What are you doing here with all the raspberry ripples? We're up the front.'

'Oh. Right.'

He teased me. 'I don't know about you. Come on, Uncle.'

'Uncle' was a nickname Steve had bestowed on me when I told him about my sister's baby. Steve led me past the teacher on duty, who pretended not to notice, while the queue automatically made room for us. All the clan – Danny, Anna, Tim Grant – were there. All except Ashley.

'Ricky was only at the back,' cried Steve.

Everyone smiled. Except Tim Grant. He'd long ago stopped glaring at me. Now he mainly ignored me. I wasn't sure if a kind of exhausted truce lay between us or Tim Grant was simply biding his time.

'Ash's been looking for you,' said Danny.

Most lunchtimes Ash and I talked together. We discussed everything but especially her love life. I expect she enjoyed discussing her love life with someone who was totally uninvolved in it. Ash was expecting Anna and Steve to have a big blow-up any day. I let her convince me.

But Anna currently had her hand in a trouser pocket on Steve's bum – and looked pretty intimate to me. Not that I know anything about it.

'And next time you see Ash,' said Anna to me, 'will you tell her to stop ignoring me. It's so childish – and we are supposed to be best friends.' She tossed her hair angrily. Anna still popped up regularly in my dreams. It was just every time I spoke to her my fantasies fell apart. She only looked like my dream woman.

'Any hassle with Ma Divvy?' Steve asked me.

'No sweat, just gave me a lecture.'

Steve smiled proudly, 'You're doing all right. See me after school and I'll fix up that newsagent's job for you.'

'Cheers, Steve,' I said gratefully.

Steve decided I had to improve my cash flow – my savings were all used up now. So he persuaded this news-agent, his 'old girl', to take me on for a trial period – two evenings a week.

Almost without thinking I piled my plate high with food. I needed a bit of soothing. And there's nothing so soothing as eating.

But as I turned round Anna snatched my plate, 'Er – please, this is the lunch of someone on a diet?'

I grinned. 'That's right, Anna. I'm on this new diet. You can eat anything you want – provided you don't swallow.'

Laughter welled up around me and Danny said, 'Give him his dinner back, Anna. He can't help being big. You've always been big, haven't you, Ricky?'

'I was seven pounds, six ounces once,' I quipped. More laughter, friendly laughter. Steve took my plate and topped it up. 'Go on, mate, pile it on. You deserve it. You're a good bloke – but just remember, no more of this at the back with the bimbos.' He patted me on the back. 'You belong up here with us now.'

One Week Later – Protecting an Investment

Steve asked me to be the look-out. I didn't mind, much. It was just Tim Grant smirking at me I didn't like. He was inside a classroom with Steve and Danny setting up a joke – definite promotion – while I was relegated to sentry duty – certain demotion in Tim Grant's eyes.

But that was pathetic. Like the joke. Would you believe they were all hiding a doll? You see, everyone's been going on about Miss Punchin – alias Punchbag – and her doll-fondling. All I've ever seen her do is look at the doll she keeps on her desk but when Tim Grant reckoned he'd seen Punchbag rocking her doll to sleep, Steve got this mighty gleam in his eye and said, 'I bet Punchbag would throw an epic wobbly if her doll went missing, wouldn't she?'

They were in Punchbag's room ten minutes, arguing madly about where to hide the doll. Then it was quieter, so perhaps this great problem had finally been solved. I hoped so. I felt a bit geeky out there, and uneasy. And if

I thought about this joke I'd probably have concluded it wasn't only moronic but also a bit sick. That was why I wasn't thinking about it.

A few seconds later, wafting up the corridor, came the cry of Punchbag. 'Who put this flour in my handbag?' I burst into the classroom to warn the doll-knappers and no-one noticed. Steve and Danny and Tim Grant were sprawled over a pair of bottles – and pouring the contents into themselves so quickly they couldn't have tasted a drop. One bottle was already empty, its top decorated by Punchbag's doll, which looked like it was doing the splits. A bleary-eyed Danny saw me and slurred, 'Pull up a bottle, Ricky. The drinks are on Punchbag. Now we know why she always kept this cupboard locked, don't we, lads?'

Steve thrust a half-empty bottle towards me. 'It's gin,' he announced.

I shuddered. 'I don't like gin.'

'Nor do we,' said Steve. 'Go on, get it down you.'

For a moment this curious scene had made me forget why I was here. Then I said quickly, 'I heard Punchbag up the corridor. She's come back from break early.'

Steve burped. They all laughed, Tim Grant especially loudly.

'Keep her talking outside,' said Steve 'and if she asks any questions tell her we're celebrating.'

More loud laughter.

'Celebrating?' I asked. 'What are you celebrating?'

'Tell you later,' snapped Tim Grant. 'You go back outside to Punchbag. This is man's work in here.'

I waited for Steve to defend me, to tell Tim Grant he couldn't talk to me like that. But apparently today he could. For Steve said nothing. Was Tim Grant back in favour and was I on the slide? But no, that was all so silly and besides, Steve was well pleased with me over what I'd planned for this Saturday.

'I'll go back then,' I said. No-one answered. I stepped outside to see Punchbag bearing down on me, her handbag bouncing furiously.

'What are you doing in my classroom?'

I jumped in front of the door, blocking it out completely – and half of the door next to it.

'I was looking for you, Miss Punchin.' I didn't sound very convincing.

'For me, why?'

'I wanted to check with you that my letter was all right.'

She started some heavy panting. Sometimes when a pupil had annoyed her she wouldn't say anything, only pant maniacally.

'Move away from my door,' she ordered.

'Why?' But as I spoke, loud laughter from inside penetrated even my flab.

'Because there's some person – or persons – still inside. Now move aside,' she cried, hauling my bulk away.

She was met at the door by Steve.

'Just as I thought,' she said. 'What are you boys doing in my room?'

'Don't worry about it,' said Steve, brushing past her

with Danny and Tim Grant sniggering behind. I followed too.

'I'll tell your form teacher about this,' cried Punchbag.

'Up yours,' muttered Steve to the accompaniment of more laughter as we legged it.

But then Punchbag let out a new sound, a sound which was a cross between a squeal and a wail. It was the kind of sound you might hear on a nature programme. This was followed by four words you'd never hear on a nature programme.

'You've stolen my doll!'

And before we knew what was happening, Punchbag was steaming towards us and screaming, 'Stop those boys!'

We ran into the art block. Steve said, 'In the bog, quick.' But before we could leap to safety, Kendal, the art teacher, had bounded in front of us. He smiled triumphantly as if he were a goalie who'd just made a tremendous save.

'Now why are you gentlemen running down my corridors?'

'Just doing a bit of jogging,' began Danny valiantly.

But it was too late. Punchbag was gasping towards us. When she saw us she had a mini-convulsion as she tried to talk, swallow and breathe all at once.

'Now take your time, Miss Punchin,' said Kendal – or, to give him his proper title, Fungus Face – patronisingly. 'I'll make sure these gentlemen don't go anywhere.'

'These boys,' spluttered Punchbag, 'have been in my classroom without permission and they've stolen . . .' she gave a kind of strangled sob while Steve nudged Danny delightedly, this was what they wanted. 'They've stolen one of my possessions.'

'This is very serious,' said Fungus Face, rubbing his hands together gleefully. I knew he was getting ready to enjoy himself.

'Tell me exactly what has been stolen, Miss Punchin.'

Steve interrupted. 'We haven't stolen anything.'

'Yes, you have,' cried Punchbag. 'You've stolen,' she started blushing, 'a doll.'

'A doll?' mused Fungus Face. 'Well – well, and is this doll yours, Miss Punchin?'

'Yes, it has great sentimental value for me.'

'Indeed.' A smile whipped across his face. I could imagine him re-telling this event in the staff room.

'And why are you young men playing with dolls?'

'We don't play with dolls,' said Steve quickly. 'It's Miss Punchin who plays with dolls. That's why we hid it, just for a joke.'

'And where did you hide Miss Punchin's . . .' he smacked his lips as if savouring the last words '. . . doll?'

'In her cupboard,' said Steve. 'May I show Miss Punchin?' he added more politely. I knew what Steve really wanted: to see Punchbag's face when she discovered her beloved perched on top of an empty gin bottle.

'No, Steven, I want a word with you trouble-makers,' said Fungus Face. 'Don't worry, Miss Punchin, I'll sort these gentlemen out for you while you check for your . . .' he couldn't resist another half-smile '. . . little doll.'

'I know it's only a doll, rather a cheap one too,' began Punchbag, 'but sometimes it's the small things that can have the most value.'

Fungus Face gave her another patronising smile, then after she'd scurried off he drew close to us. Like all teachers he reeked of stale coffee and a permanent coffee cup rim glistened on his beard. I thought he was the most repulsive teacher in the school – and the most unfair, as now, when he directed his whole lecture at me. Just looking at me sent his voice all cold and hard. But whenever he looked at Steve or Danny he started making with the 'I'm a lad too' comments and cracking jokes about his school days. Then it was back to me and the heavy lecture. Each time he did that he got me more irritated. Either he was telling all of us off – or none of us. He wasn't being fair. Finally, it was back to Steve and Danny and his jovial manner. 'Okay, lads. I know you didn't mean any harm, you just wanted to liven things up. I know, because when I was your age I was just like you and that wasn't as many years ago as you might think,' he chuckled reminiscently while I yawned. But he wasn't looking at me. He obviously didn't like to imagine he was ever like me.

'So, lads,' he went on, 'I'm letting you off now but I warn you next time you get up to any mischief I'll cut your left legs off – all of them.' I started counting my legs, then asked in a puzzled voice, 'How many left legs you got, Steve? I've only got one. How about you, Danny?'

A little joke and a little protest at the way he'd been

creeping around Steve and Danny and going on at me, that's all. But as I was about to discover, a most dangerous joke.

For while Steve and Danny – and even Tim Grant – grinned away at my comments, Fungus Face had turned rigid with anger. And when he spoke to me, not even his lips seemed to move.

'I try and be reasonable with you and this is how you behave. Well, Hodgson, I think you need a sharp lesson and I'm going to make sure you get it. I'm sending you straight to Mr Weedle.' He glared at me. The sight of me seemed to fire up fresh hatred in him. 'No, I'm not, I'm sending you straight to the Headmaster. It is time he knew about your behaviour and dealt with you.' I gaped at him, totally stunned. Steve and Danny were obviously really shocked too.

'Oh come on,' began Danny. 'You can't send him to the Headmaster just for making a joke.'

'Oh can't I, Danny?' said Fungus Face, all aggressively.

Steve tried another approach.

'Sir, you're a really good bloke. Everyone likes you, respects you. You'd never do anything unfair.'

Fungus Face rolled back his shoulders, drinking in Steve's praise.

'I am a fair man,' he pronounced. He was wavering. Then I sneezed. He glanced my way and that did it. You could say, a sneeze decided my fate.

'But in Richard Hodgson's case I have no choice. His behaviour has shown a marked deterioration this term and his appearance before the Headmaster is long overdue. I will take him over now.'

'But sir . . .' began Steve.

'And if there's any more backchat you three will be accompanying Hodgson.'

The backchat ceased instantly, just a look of sympathy from Danny, a typically blank gaze from Tim Grant and a mouthed message from Steve which I didn't understand.

I didn't quite understand how I'd ended up in the bad boys' waiting corner by Slap-Head's office either. The last few minutes already seemed hazy and slightly out of focus. And it had all happened so quickly.

I watched Slap-Head's secretaries buzzing past me. None looked at me. Not even a quick, curious glance. I suppose bad boys were such a common species over here you gave up noticing them. And now I'd joined the bad boys.

I had a tight, pulsating pain in my stomach. I just wanted to get the encounter over. Steve told me once, that Slap-Head always kept you waiting – that was part of the torture – the worst part. I must try and think of something else, something happy. Like this Saturday. Would you believe I'm having a few friends around? For my jailers are off visiting sister and baby Paul, now they're out of hospital, and they will be gone for a whole evening. I said I couldn't join them – too much revision – and they believed me. Actually, it's been really good lately, for Mum's X-ray gaze has been concentrated on my nephew. Mum did say to me yesterday that she was worried about me working all Saturday night – and why don't I invite Ashley around for a cup of coffee.

If only Mum knew! But never – not in her wildest dreams – could she imagine what I'd got planned for Saturday night. I can't quite believe it myself. I mean, me being free to invite all my friends around without any interruptions or explanations. I'll be able to meet my mates at the door, prepare them drinks, tell them, 'Don't stand up, sit yourself down, make yourself at home . . .'

I was so lost in the dream I didn't hear a faint tapping on the window behind me. It was only when the tapping grew slightly louder I whirled round. Steve was miming at me to open a window. He also had a finger over his mouth. So I kept facing the front while my left hand (yes, I'm left-handed) curved behind me, searching for the handle. I groped and found and tugged. It was one of those windows with shutters and they all snapped open so sharply I felt sure someone must have heard. But my little noise was drowned by great cackles of laughter coming from this goldfish bowl of a room where the secretaries lived. For the moment the coast was clear. Steve spoke in a low, urgent whisper. 'Don't turn around, just listen. Punchbag is going to tell Slap-Head she was wrong about you stealing the doll and that she'd put the doll in the cupboard herself.'

'But why is she going to do that?' I hissed.

' 'Cause we warned her that if she doesn't do that you'll tell Slap-Head about her secret drink supply. You should see Punchbag, she's well scared.'

I didn't reply. This all seemed a bit nasty.

Steve guessed my thoughts. 'Now don't get soft. Teachers are always trying to get things on us – for once we've got something on them. If Slap-Head found out about Punchbag being an alkie she'd be flung out, right away. So we've got her well suckered. She'll be over any minute; then Slap-Head will have to apologise to you for wrongful arrest and probably throw out Fungus Face's charges too.' His tone changed, 'You don't want to go before Slap-Head if you can help it. He can be mighty vicious.'

I darted a glance at Steve between the gaps of the shutters. This conversation seemed oddly unreal. It was as if I was playing a part in a film set in a prison. And it was me who was behind bars. That was the most unreal part.

'Anyone looking?' asked Steve.

'No.'

'Put your hand to the window then, quick.'

Into my sweaty paw Steve plonked a bar of chocolate.

'I know how much you like chocolate.'

'Cheers, Steve.'

'Sorry there's a bit missing. Got a bit hungry coming over here. Anyway, mate, I'm going to see what's keeping Punchbag. Keep smiling. Think of us lot having a piss-up round your house on Saturday.'

'Yeah, right, Steve.'

He was being really good to me again. And I couldn't help feel a little tremor of pleasure about that. It also reminded me . . . 'Steve, what were you celebrating in Punchbag's room?'

'My freedom.'

'Your what?'

'Well, I . . .'

Steve dived away, for he'd seen a door opening. Slap-Head's door.

Nothing came out of the door at first, not even a bat. But then a dark figure with a black cape wrapped completely around it swirled past me and into the goldfish bowl. And inside was Ma Divvy, my form teacher. I could see their lips moving, I was sure they were talking about me. I ached, not so much with pain as loneliness. Why wasn't someone here with me? Then it wouldn't seem so bad. Why wasn't Steve here – or Ashley?

Ashley – what a day you picked to skive off! Ashley – please be here with me – even if it's just for a minute. For in that one minute you'd give me such a shot of life I could face anything afterwards. Ashley, Slap-Head's addressing two backs now: Ma Divvy and Punchbag. It must be me they're talking about. And Punchbag is shuffling around Slap-Head. Is she pleading for me? Ashley, make me laugh, tell me one of your long, funny stories. Ashley, how come I've ended up here all on my own?

Then Slap-Head is out, skimming past his saluting secretaries but still not disentangled from a bleating Punchbag.

'But I must insist, Headmaster, that Richard Hodgson

is not punished. For he is completely innocent. It is all my fault, my fault entirely,' and she kept catching the edge of his cloak as if he were a great god – or devil.

Steve had done what he promised: got Punchbag totally scared. And as a result, Punchbag was now doing exactly what Steve wanted. I watched Slap-Head patting Punchbag on the back, then he said, 'Your desire for honesty and fair play does you much credit, Miss Punchin.' His tone was warm. I started to breathe again. A second year edged behind Slap-Head and winked at me. I jauntily returned the wink. Steve had saved me.

But then, without any warning, Slap-Head ran forward, pounced and hoisted his victim right up into the air. One day when aliens make films about us they'll include footage of a rampaging Headmaster. And they'll wonder how Slap-Head could see a second year, who was out of his eye-shot. And perhaps they'll show a close-up of those thin, second-year legs waggling unhappily in the air or that second-year face drained of colour and life. They might call in the 'Law of the School' and end with Slap-Head's high, headmasterish roar, 'Why are you wearing trainers?'

'I don't know, sir.'

Slap-Head hurled the second year away from him, the way you and I might hurl a ball at skittles.

'Change now, boy,' he ordered.

And then he picked up his conversation with Punchbag as if nothing had happened.

'But Miss Punchin, there are other matters I need to

discuss – with –' he jutted his chin at me as he whisked back into his lair.

One second year half-limped, half-ran away, one per-spiring fifth year stared down at his trainers, non-white shirt, absent tie. I tried to do up my top button, it's hard to do when you hand's shaking so much. Across from me Punchbag was shaking too. 'I did try,' she called.

A voice from the bowels of Slap-Head's office bade me enter.

I shakily stepped forward.

'Good luck,' croaked Punchbag.

And before I slunk into the torture chamber I gave her a faint smile. I wanted her to know I'd never tell about her secret gin supply. And if she gained comfort from a doll, what did it matter? We all need something. I smiled at her again. But I think she was too terrified to receive any messages from me.

Inside there were no racks on the wall, in fact no instruments of torture were visible except for the man in the black cape. And the walls. They were vomit yellow. Highly appropriate. And although I'd obviously never been here in my boffin days, it all seemed oddly familiar. Perhaps I'd visited here in a nightmare, long ago. If only I could remember what had happened to me.

Slap-Head stared me into a chair. It was like sitting on a rock – only harder. Then he leant back in his round, swivelley chair-throne and watched me squirm. He didn't talk at first, just stared menacingly.

Up close he looked younger, in fact his face had a hollow, unformed look about it. Thick rolls of flesh grew beneath his chin though and he was completely bald, save for one particle of hair, which was parted across the middle of his head. It looked as if a piece of Shredded Wheat had landed on him.

Then he spoke. His voice was oddly high-pitched, a sort of metallic bark. 'Do you know why you are here?'

'I think so, sir.' I was grovelling, quite unashamedly. Some old habits die hard.

'Now, explain to me what you think my job is.'

I hadn't expected questions, just a lecture. Of course my mind froze up.

'Er – you run the school.'

'Yes, I run the school but on what?'

'Pardon?'

'What enables me to run the school?'

'Teachers,' I said moronically.

This was clearly the wrong answer.

'What enables me to hire teachers?'

I was sweating. What was he going on about?

'Money?' I ventured. He pounced on the word.

'Money, of course, money. I run the school on the money I'm given by thousands of tax-payers. You might say I'm here to protect their investment,' and his eyes bore down on me, 'and to take appropriate action when their investment is not paying off.' He leaned forward. 'Your report card says you are not giving our tax-payers value for money. In fact,' he hissed, 'you are wasting their funding.'

I shrank down in my chair.

'Please explain why you are wasting your time and their money.'

A phone buzzed. 'One minute,' he yapped into it before slamming it back down. 'So then,' his tone became brisk, 'are you going to get down to some solid work?' He paused and shuffled through some sheets. He was looking for my name. He didn't even know who I was. Even now. Finally he found it and continued. 'So, Hodgson, are you going to justify our investment in you and make a maximum effort?'

He didn't even look up, he was already folding up his notes on me. As soon as I said 'Yes, sir, I will be a good boy,' this interview would be at an end. To Slap-Head, I was no more than a bolt that had come loose. He'd now applied the appropriate pressure, leaving me all tightened up again. Well, suddenly I didn't want to be so quickly dismissed. I wanted him to ask at least one question, to be a little curious about me. Me.

He looked up. 'I can't hear your answer, Hodgson. Are you prepared to direct yourself towards your maximum potential?'

All at once I noticed his one bit of hair had slipped down towards his shoulder. It dangled there now like a plait. He looked suddenly absurd. This whole charade was absurd. And I found the courage to say: 'In answer to your question, I don't know how hard I'll be working. I've been re-thinking the whole idea of school work and its value lately.'

His lower lip went in under his teeth and he bared his teeth at me before answering.

'I'm afraid then, Hodgson, you leave me only one alternative. Suspension.'

'What?'

'I will tolerate no pupil in my school who is not prepared to work.' He added airily, 'You're suspended until further notice.'

His words pounded into me like a fist knocking my breath away. I was gasping for air. I was terrified.

'As you are a Year Eleven boy,' he continued, 'this suspension could lead to,' he licked the word before he spat it out at me, 'expulsion.'

Now the room was shrinking. Those hideous walls moved in nearer and nearer. And I was shrinking too. Only Slap-Head grew to giant proportions. I watched his now huge hand as it pulled at my card and his voice bellowed in my ears. 'I see from your card that your mother is at home all day. I will ring her now and inform her of my decision.'

I twisted around in my chair. Great rivers of sweat were forming on my brow. 'Don't ring my mother,' I whimpered. I couldn't bear that. Not now when she was so happy about the baby. Not – before Saturday.

'It is essential your mother knows as soon as possible.' He pressed a button, 'Miss Knight, get me Richard Hodgson's mother on the line, please.'

Cowering before him, and feeling quite dizzy with fear, I pleaded, 'Please don't suspend me. Please don't.'

164

He rubbed his hand up and down on my form card.

'But you're not prepared to work here.'

'Yes, I will work,' I screamed. 'I will work. I promise – only don't suspend me.'

He picked up his phone and said, just a trifle too casually, 'Cancel that call, Karen,' then he pushed my report card away just a trifle too quickly and even before he said, 'All right, you have one last chance,' I knew I'd been conned.

It had all been one great firework of a deception. One mighty display of power, to scare me into submission. He'd got something on me, my fear of expulsion – and used it to the full. Steve was right. School was just one long power struggle and I'd just been well suckered.

His phone buzzed again. He listened, nodded and exclaimed. 'He's what?' His voice became heavy. 'Yes, then I will see him now.' He replaced his phone and smiled at me. Instantly his eyes disappeared. 'I hope I don't have to see you again, Hodgson – and will you tell the next pupil to see me?'

He smiled again, a smile of victory. I stood up, bathed in sweat and itching all over with anger. I wanted to shout and yell, 'You faker, that was a cheap, nasty trick.' But I didn't, of course. I crept outside to face Tim Grant.

He had his hands down his pockets and was chewing gum.

'What sort of mood's he in?' he asked casually.

'Bad. But what are you doing here?'

'That new supply, Spam, threw a board rubber at me. I

threw it back. It was a brilliant shot.' He started grinning idiotically. He was obviously very pleased with himself. I knew he felt he'd caught me up.

'Catch you after,' he said as he swaggered inside.

He wouldn't swagger out again of course, or would he? Well, surely he couldn't dissolve away as quickly as me.

I bunged my hands down my jacket pockets and touched a black, gooey liquid. It was the remains of Steve's chocolate – or was it my guts?

Still feeling winded by the whole sorry episode I made for the back field. I needed a moment alone, a chance to get my strength back. But suddenly my strength surged back all on its own. I saw Ashley sauntering into school, quite unperturbed by the fact that she was three hours late. I sped towards her.

'And why aren't you in your lessons, young man?' she said, impersonating Fungus Face's voice remarkably well.

'And why aren't you?' I replied, impersonating Fungus Face remarkably ineptly.

'I asked you first.'

'All right. I was sent to Slap-Head.'

'Why?' Concern lit up her face.

'Long story. Basically, Fungus Face sent me for telling a joke.'

'Trust him. He's really got it in for you, hasn't he? So what happened?'

'Nothing really. Slap-Head gave me a grilling, and threatened to expel me.'

'He did that to me. Threatened to ring my dad up at work.'

'I fell for it, I'm afraid, and I promised to be a good boy.'

She stroked my chin. 'Aaah, poor Ricky, you look so sad and sorry for yourself. Well, don't be. He's really sly, everyone falls for his tricks, that's why he's a Headmaster.'

'But he didn't even try and understand why I was there. He obviously sees me and all the boys who get sent to him as anarchists and rebels. He doesn't realise that most of us aren't rebelling against anything – we're just trying to say, "Look, I'm here." But school won't let you do that.'

Ash was smiling at me. 'Who'd have thought it, you being sent to Slap-Head. How you've changed.'

'You reckon?'

'Oh yes – you're just a completely different person now. Completely different.' She said it so approvingly, I felt embarrassed.

'All right,' I said. 'Your turn now. What's your excuse for being three hours late?'

'My rabbit died.'

'What?'

'Don't you dare laugh. I've had him since I was eight and this morning . . .' she shuddered, 'Poor little thing. It really upset me. I cried.'

'Aaarh.'

'I was crying when my dad and his secretary popped home to pick up some papers.'

'Did he give you a rollicking?'

'No, he was really nice about it. Went out with me

when I buried Topsy – and was really nice. Almost too nice. I mean, he even drove me to school and he never does that.'

Ashley giggled. 'Oh dear, I think we'd better move.'

One of the secretaries in the goldfish bowl was knocking furiously away on the window and scowling at us.

'Why can't she mind her own business?' I said. 'What's it to do with her?'

'You sounded just like Steve when you said that.'

I blushed at the surprise compliment and continued talking in the same tone. 'And there's no way I'm going to Fungus Face's lesson now, after all that's happened.'

'Well, look, if we walk really slowly over to the art block, by the time we get there, the lesson will have finished.' She squeezed my shoulder, 'Cheer up, everything's going to be all right.'

I glanced down at her hands. Her finger-nails, as always, glowed.

'What colour are they today then?'

'What?'

'Your finger-nails.'

'Oh, whatever colour you like.'

'A sort of reddy-gold, aren't they?'

'Supposed to be. Only some of it's chipped off already. Takes hours to put it on and then it comes off straight away.' She laughed. 'Gosh, this is a really interesting conversation, isn't it?'

'Whatever you say is interesting, Ashley,' I said, but I spoke as if I was messing about.

'I was going to ring you last night,' said Ashley.

'You should have.'

'Yes, the trouble was I rang my penfriend to wish her a happy birthday and I fell asleep.'

'Well, she sounds a good conversationalist.'

'No, no,' Ashley started laughing again. 'No, I never actually got through to her. I kept ringing her but she was always engaged and while I was waiting on the line I fell asleep.'

'Hey, Ash!' called a voice from the classroom we were walking past.

'All right, Mark,' she called back.

Some other people smiled at her. She gave them all epic smiles in return. Ashley's more generous with her smiles than anyone else I know. In fact there's never any holding back with Ashley, she seems to spill herself willingly on whoever's around.

Just as we reached Fungus Face's, the bell rang.

'Well, what a shame. I mean, I'm so sorry,' said Ashley.

'I'll wait back here a bit,' I said. 'I don't want to meet Fungus Face now.'

'I think I'll give him a miss too,' said Ashley. 'I took in some of my designs to show him once. All he asked about was the paper I'd used.'

'Typical,' I said.

So we both waited down by the loos. Even there we could hear the noisy clatter of stools being put on the desks. Fungus Face insists on them being put up after lessons. Then Fungus Face marched out. He didn't see us. But Mouse, who was following him, did. He came over. 'I hear you are having some friends around on Saturday.'

'That's true,' I said guardedly, waiting for the sarky response.

'Well, I hope you will invite me,' mumbled Mouse and before I could reply he'd darted away.

'Don't tell me Mouse is turning cool as well,' said Ashley. 'We'll have no boffins left soon.'

'That's right,' I said, intrigued and pleased by what Mouse had said – and I certainly would invite him round on Saturday.

A small crowd started to form round me. They'd heard of my facing Slap-Head and wanted to know every gory detail. But Steve quickly ushered them away – and Ashley too.

'He'll talk to you pondlife later. He's talking to his mates first,' said Steve, and he plonked me into Fungus Face's room just as though he were moving a checker on to another square. Danny closed the door behind us.

'Come on then, spill,' said Steve. 'Spare us nothing. Did Punchbag do her stuff?'

'Oh yeah, you'd got her well shook up. She was really praising me up. But Slap-Head also got hold of my record card. Then he threatened to suspend me and said he was going to ring my moth – old dear.'

'Yeah, typical Slap-Head,' Steve sighed reminiscently. 'I must have been in there a million times. Every time he threatens to ring my old man and never does it. Until one day he does. And my old man goes give him a good belting; that's all he needs. Trust my old man.'

Steve stared at me thoughtfully. 'You look a bit groggy, mate. Still, the first time's always a shocker, isn't it, Danny?' he winked at Danny.

'Didn't see Grantie, did you?' asked Danny.

'Yeah, he went in as I came out.'

'I'll go and see if he's out yet,' said Danny.

'Tell you, Ricky, it was well wicked the way Grantie just threw that board rubber at Spam. Then Steve pretends he's got this bomb in his desk. Spam was wetting himself. Hasn't been a bad morning, has it?' he concluded.

'Go and get us a ciggie, mate,' said Steve, 'and if you see Ash . . .'

Danny grinned, 'Leave Ash to me,' he said as he left.

'What's this about Ash?' I said immediately.

'It's what I tried to tell you before,' said Steve. 'I'm a free man. I chucked Anna last night.'

'You did?'

'Well, don't cry about it. It was no big deal. She was round my house doing her homework and I thought, I've had enough of this. So I ditched her.'

'What did she do?'

'She said, "Fair enough" and left.'

I couldn't believe that. After all those weeks of Steve and Anna going round together, Steve suddenly calls it off and Anna just says, 'Fair enough.' There must be more to it than that. But Steve's face was expressionless.

'You seem a bit shocked by my news,' said Steve.

'I am, a bit,' I replied.

'Anyway, you're always going on about Ashley so I thought I'd give her another chance and I'm going to take her round your house on Saturday.'

I rushed to my feet. 'Shall we go?' I hoped my voice didn't sound shaky.

'Yeah, I suppose you're starving as usual. Come on then, Uncle.' He made for the door.

'Oh, one thing, Steve,' I said. 'Aren't we forgetting something?'

'What?' he looked puzzled.

'This.' I turned towards the stools and with one mighty blow sent them all crashing to the floor like a row of dominoes.

'Wow, you lad,' said Steve. 'We're going to have to watch you.' He said it only half-jokingly. 'I don't blame you either,' he added, 'you must be really mad with Fungus Face.' But it wasn't Fungus Face I'd thought of as I sent those stools flying.

That night, a phone call I'd been dreading.

'Guess what?' Ashley's voice was just as I'd imagined it, all bright and excited. 'Steve's invited –'

'Steve's invited you round my house on Saturday.'

'Spoilsport. I wanted to surprise you. But isn't it amazing?'

'Amazing.'

'Of course, Anna reckons she chucked Steve and Steve says he chucked her, but what does all that matter? What matters is, it's all happening just as you said. You knew all along, didn't you?'

'Yes, I knew.'

'You're so clever, Ricky. You remember that night you came back to my house and said to me – right off the top of your head too – "Ashley, forever wilt thou love and it will never pass into nothingness"? Well, I've thought of that so often. And Ricky, it really helped me.' A pause. 'Ricky, you still there?'

'I'm here,' I said. 'And I'm just so happy for you. You deserve lots of happiness.' That wasn't a lie. I was happy for her. Of course I was sad for myself. For when Steve comes back on the scene, I'll have to exit, as she won't need me any more. But that's just selfishness on my part. Ashley deserves the best. And the best isn't a fat guy whose face looks like it's been hit with a brick. The best is Steve. Now she's got the best. Happy ending.

'Here's to Saturday then,' said Ashley. 'I know it's going to be really special.'

'To Saturday,' I echoed flatly.

'See you then, Ricky.'

'Goodbye, Ashley.'

Strange Powers and Forces

Tonight there was a light in Ashley's eyes I'd never seen before. It appeared every time she smiled at me. Like now.

'Am I the first to arrive?' she asked.

'Well, apart from Steve and Danny who've been here helping me set things up, you're certainly my first party guest my . . .' I couldn't concentrate, not with her looking at me like that, her face all lit up.

'But don't you look good tonight,' she said, squeezing closer to me. 'Mind if I kiss you?'

'Delighted,' I replied, shaking with anticipation. 'But what about Steve . . .?'

'Seeing you tonight makes me forget – whoever it was you just mentioned. Oh, Richard, you rock my world.'

Her lips touched mine, they dissolved instantly and I could feel her . . .'

'You gone to sleep up there?' called Steve.

I shook myself guiltily and before I could answer he

174

went on, 'I'm going to ring up Grantie now, tell him about the toga party.'

'Oh yeah, right,' I said, still not quite out of my day dream. 'I've nearly finished up here.'

Actually, I hadn't even started. Steve and Danny had sent me upstairs to take the sheets off all the beds.

'If they want to do it, they can do it on the floor,' Steve had said. Typical of me to spend the time lying on a bed, imagining things that would never happen.

I tore round frantically de-bedding each room. I did my room last. Then just before going downstairs, I went and stood right in front of my mirror – boldly, defiantly, bravely. Tonight it couldn't get me, for tonight I'd covered it up with a thick blue towel as I had no intention of my party night being spoilt by any miserable, lying mirrors. I've even managed to buy myself a whole new set of clothes this afternoon without looking at myself once. I let Steve and Danny be my eyes. It'd all been a bit of an emergency too.

I squared up to my towelled mirror and raised two fingers at it. This is one party you can't ruin.

Who'd have thought it – a former boffin now entertaining twenty guests. Here surely was proof positive that I'd climbed my way into a new world. It might have been a slow ascent at first but tonight I'd surely reached the summit.

I stifled a laugh. The towel covering my mirror was Mum's. She'd be so furious. She hated anyone even breathing near her towel. And as for downstairs, she'd throw a fit if she saw the lounge with all her boring furniture – which was everything except the settee – relegated to the edges. She'd hate, too, the way everything now looked so airy and full of space. But I've been careful, Mum. We locked all your valuables away – 'Anything not nailed down will be stolen,' Steve had joked.

Oh, my poor mum. You'll never know about tonight and in a way that makes me sad. I'd really like to tell you. And I would if I thought there was any way I could get you to understand what tonight means to me.

Downstairs, I passed Steve in the hallway, still on the phone to Tim Grant. I heard him say, 'I went ape, mate, when I heard Ricky hadn't told you about this toga party . . . yeah, yeah, that's right, mate, round here tonight and no-one's being let in who's not wearing a toga.'

I marvelled at how Steve could be grinning all over his face and yet still keep his voice so serious. Tim Grant was certainly being well set up tonight.

In the lounge Danny was whacking my stereo with a baseball bat.

'Hey, Ricky,' he called, 'how can you get this to go up a few thousand watts?'

'I don't think it will go up any louder,' I said, 'one of the speakers has gone and it's quite old and . . .'

'But it must go up louder than this. I'll give it another go in a minute.'

He swished his baseball bat about in the air. 'This bat here, Ricky, is an excellent weapon of defence for parties, not that I'm expecting any trouble tonight. Not with a small house-party like this one. It's just house-parties are pretty rare and if the word gets around . . .'

'But how will it? Everyone's sworn to secrecy.'

'Yeah, yeah, but these things still get about,' he said mysteriously. 'Steve's a dab hand with the old baseball bat.' He went on, 'You should see him, he loves bouncing people out, can get really violent about it.' He paused. 'Don't suppose Steve has said anything to you?'

'About what?'

'Well, whenever Steve messes Grantie about, it's a sure sign he's uptight about something.'

'Oh well, he hasn't said anything . . .'

'No, didn't suppose he would. Steve's a man of few words.' Danny jumped to his feet. 'He only knows a few.' He grinned. 'Still, Ash'll be here any minute. She should keep him busy.'

A sharp needle plunged itself through my insides. It happened every time I thought of Ash and Steve together. I knew the cause: jealousy, pure and simple. But knowing that doesn't make it any the less painful somehow.

'At least we haven't got Anna here tonight,' Danny said. 'Can you imagine the vibes with her and Ash at each other's throats? It's bad enough at school when if you talk to one, the other goes all huffy.' Danny resumed his bat-swishing. 'And I can't handle all that. I don't see why they can't be sensible about it and just knock each other's teeth out. That's what I'd do. I'd . . .'

His voice fell away. Steve was grinning in the doorway. 'Grantie's well suckered,' he said. 'I left him wittering on about borrowing his mum's sheets. I tell you, it's going to be a killer-laugh when he rolls in here.'

Danny was right. Something must be bugging Steve, for I'd never seen him so hyped up. I watched him bounding around the lounge, shouting, 'Come on – it's party-time or no-time. Let's get this party swinging.' He leapt into the kitchen, scooping up a pile of cans. Danny did the same.

'A tre – mend – ous party,' said Steve to me, 'is where the drink never runs out. This looks like a tre – mend – ous party.'

There was certainly stacks of drink – Steve and Danny had bought it, I'd paid for it. This afternoon I'd also bought masses of food. If I say so myself it was a mighty spread.

'This party must be setting Ricky back a bit, don't you reckon, Steve?' said Danny, who now had as many cans in his arms as Steve.

'Yeah, it must have cost you a fortune,' said Steve, balancing a can on his shoulders.

'Well, I borrowed some money on my job at Bunce's,' I said. 'I promised them I'll go in every day next week, rather than just Thursdays and Fridays. My mum'll go crazy when I tell her but . . .'

'Why should she worry?' snapped Steve. 'You're bringing in money and that's what it's all about. I could work all night down the garage for all my old lady would care.' He began edging towards the door, backwards. 'No, as soon as your mum sees the money you're making, she'll be happy and . . .'

'You'll never make it through the door without dropping any,' interrupted Danny.

'Oh yeah, want to bet? Watch this, mate.' He eased out of the doorway, cans all remaining intact but then he started trying to turn round. At once, a few cans escaped, then Danny pushed him and all the rest of his cans escaped, then he pushed Danny and all Danny's cans joined his on the floor.

I watched them scrambling and pushing each other, fighting over the cans as if there weren't hundreds more in the kitchen. Finally they lined up all the cans by the settee.

Steve threw a can at me, 'Come on, get drinking.'

'Right.' This was the bit I'd been dreading. I never wanted to drink more than one pint of lager as I hated the heavy gassy feeling it left and the way I wanted to burp all the time. But tonight I knew Steve wouldn't let me get away with only one pint of lager!

'Come on, Danny,' cried Steve. 'Get the music up. This is a party, for God's sake.'

'I've been trying,' said Danny, belting his baseball bat down on the stereo so hard the whole room shook.

I was about to suggest that this possibly wasn't the best way to operate our stereo, when suddenly Steve and Danny were on their feet – dancing and pretending to head-butt each other. Steve yelled, 'Get in here, Ricky,' and as I went over, the three of us formed a kind of dancing scrum. Sweat was already pouring down Steve's face and every so often he did a kind of backflip on to the cans, threw some lager over himself and head-butted his way into us again, while Danny kept looking at me and nodding at Steve and grinning.

The doorbell rang.

'The party's starting,' hissed Steve. 'Go for it, Ricky.'

'You want me to answer it?' I suddenly felt absurdly panicky.

'It's your party,' said Steve, grinning. 'You check out the door, we'll get the atmosphere going in here.'

As I approached the front door the doorbell rang again. I drank in its sweet alien sound, before opening the door on Ashley. Behind her the wind roared and raged and seemed to blow her inside. She was smiling broadly at me. But there was no light in her eyes. And she wasn't dressed as I'd imagined – rather she had on this tight red skirt and a blouse which you could see through. There was a lot to see – but I was too embarrassed to look properly. I looked again at those eyes, a quick check action. No, no light there, not that I could really tell. For she'd coated her face with so much black she'd almost camouflaged her eyes away.

'Hello, darlin',' she said. 'How's everything going?'

'Fine. It's good to see you, Ashley.'

She put down the brown carrier bag she'd been holding and briefly displayed its contents, two bottles of wine.

'These are for you – to wish you a mega party.'

'Ash, that's very generous of you.'

'Very generous of my dad actually,' said Ashley. But she spoke really flatly.

'That money was his, his . . .' I think she was about to tell me something. But instead she changed the subject. 'I haven't a clue what the wine tastes like, by the way. But it's got this really long foreign name so it must be good . . . hey come here a minute . . .' Her hands touched my shoulders. I shivered. Then she started pulling out the sleeves on my shirt. 'These look better if they're pushed out a bit . . . there now, you look sorted.' I shivered again. That's what she said to me when I'd been imagining her . . . now she was stroking my hand.

'You're shaking. Not nervous about tonight, are you?'

'Yes, no, it's only . . .' I hardly trusted myself to speak. 'It's just so good to see you, Ash.'

'Oh you babe,' she said softly and she put her arms around me and hugged me, just like I'd imagined – well no – not exactly. This was a lighter, gentler hug but I still closed my eyes. I'd long ago stopped hearing Steve and Danny calling me as they thumped about in the lounge. What did I care about any of that? I was hugging my girlfriend. For this moment she was anyhow.

The hug was ending and I opened my eyes – only to be dazzled by this great white light; it engulfed Ash and me like a giant spotlight. Where had this light come from? From me? Had I conjured it up? Was it a kind of physical manifestation of my feelings for Ash? I began to get excited. But then I saw Ash turn and blink through the spotlight at voices which were calling out, 'We know what you're doing.'

'Who are they?' Ash asked.

I shook my head. Then car doors banged and these blokes came strutting towards us, waving cans in the air as if they were flags. The car headlights remained beamed over us. There were seven of them and only one of me but I said as defiantly as I could, 'I'm afraid this is a private party.' But the tallest guy just muttered, 'Steve there?'

'Yes,' I faltered.

And at that moment Steve burst out. 'There we are, trying to create atmosphere in there and you keep everyone out . . .' then he saw the extra guests and I waited for him to tell them to get lost but instead he greeted every one of them. They worked up the garage with him and he had invited them all to my party – and forgotten to tell me.

The tall guy said, 'When we arrived, these two were at it, in the doorway,' pointing at Ash and me, and I flushed with pride until Steve pretended to be angry. And I knew he wasn't bothered at all – insulting really. Anyhow, Steve gave Ash this great smacker of a kiss in the hallway and we all watched – for in a way it was like a demonstration. Then he ruffled Ash's hair, the way he sometimes ruffled mine or Tim Grant's, saying, 'So how goes it tonight?' and before she could reply, Steve was outside with Danny exclaiming over the 10,000 spotlights on the front of the car.

I watched Ash hovering on the edge of the Lads' conversation, a big smile plastered clumsily across her face. Once or twice she'd whisper to me things like, 'Why do blokes with really thin legs always wear tight trousers?'

182

and she'd point, giggling, at one of the Lads. But most of the time she was trying to catch Steve's eye, while great gusts of icy wind tore around us. No wonder she looked so famished with the cold.

I sneaked inside and found this old coat of my sister's in the cupboard under the stairs. I brought it out and offered it to Ash. 'Oh how sweet of you but I'm all right – I've got my tan to keep me warm.' But she let me put it round her shoulders and she smiled and giggled but she still looked cold – even when we went inside.

The Lads helped themselves to booze and food – before I even had time to say 'Help yourselves.' I think Steve introduced each one to me. But really they were just one person $\times$ 7 or, as Mouse might say 1^7. They were dressed so identically they could have used each other for mirrors.

There was then a rather awkward conversation, about nothing in particular, until one of the seven said something about 'talent' and then peered down Ash's top. I thought Steve might get mad but he didn't and soon everyone was staring at Ash, all smiling the same kind of leer. I had a look too.

I'd never realised Ash's breasts were quite so beautiful – or that they moved so much. But then I'd only stolen furtive looks at a few breasts in magazines and they of course were quite still.

At first I don't think Ash minded all the peering. She even said, 'I'm not ashamed of anything I've got. Anyhow you've got 'em too, its just ours are a lot puffier.'

She was right. How could anyone be ashamed of

something so exquisite? But the jokes went on – ones about melons and sucking – you probably know the sort of thing and they became really quite nasty, I thought. And it was as if everyone was angry with Ash for having such beautiful breasts.

I was actually relieved when the doorbell went again. No-one waited for me to answer it this time, they just charged for the door, all psyched up now. This proved unfortunate for the caller. A figure in a toga.

'You're early,' cried Steve indignantly at Tim Grant. And then he yelled 'Get 'im, lads' as Tim Grant – realising in one second he'd been 'had', tried to leg it.

But it's hard to run in a toga (not that I've ever tried) and Tim Grant was soon carried into the lounge on a tide of shouting and sweat.

'I knew you were all suckering me,' he hollered pathetically as Steve hauled him up into the air.

Soon I lost sight of him, only his toga kept bobbing in and out of view. And not even the doorbell ringing again interrupted this ceremony. I opened the door on more mates of Steve's whom I'd never seen. They surged straight into the fray.

Ash cried, 'Oh, leave him alone. It's not fair. It's twenty-to-one,' but no-one heard her lone voice. They didn't see or hear me either, they were too full of a kind of crazy energy to see anything except their victim.

As I watched them crashing around my lounge, a feeling of desperate panic started rising inside me. What was happening here? I'd imagined my party being full of music and drink and laughter and people being high. I'd looked forward to being high myself as all the usual limits disappeared – but this chaotic sprawl, this mess wasn't what I'd planned. And all these strangers . . . and it was only nine o'clock. What would happen when more guests poured in and everyone became more drunk? I didn't know and I didn't want to guess either. All I knew was I'd opened my house up to strange powers and forces which I'd never understood, only feared.

Finally, Tim Grant managed to break away and run behind the settee. He lay there cowering in the corner, as Ashley screamed, 'Oh, can't you leave him alone!'

'Yeah, all right, break it up,' said Steve.

The bundle retreated and the music became the main noise again.

'Oh, you're all so cruel,' said Ash.

'Nah, it was only a joke,' said Steve, 'wasn't it, Grantie?'

Tim Grant smiled through clenched teeth. He looked so pitiful, I said, 'I've got some clothes upstairs if you want to – er . . .'

'No, no, he'll pull more birds like that,' said one of the second squad of Lads. (I hadn't even been introduced to them.)

But Tim Grant grunted, 'I might as well' so ungraciously, I knew he was grateful to me. He cautiously skirted past the semi-circle of Lads, then swaggered upstairs.

He sat on my mattress, tense, unsmiling, suspicious.

'I've got this pale yellow top and . . .'

'Yeah, yeah, anything,' he said brusquely. 'I'm not

staying long.' He plunged into my top and I couldn't help noticing how his muscles positively swung out of my sleeves. I remembered Mouse saying of Tim Grant, 'He's got muscles where other people have only got brains.' But despite myself, I was impressed – and envious – at his swelling muscles. I said so.

He blushed proudly. 'It hasn't been easy. Takes a while. You only went to one body-building class, didn't you?'

'I couldn't take the pain,' I confessed.

'No pain, no gain,' he recited, putting on my jeans. 'Plenty of room there,' he said, grinning as he waggled his hand up and down the part of my jeans normally packed with flab. Then he faced the mirror. 'What's this doing here?' he said, flinging the towel on to the floor.

For a second I saw my reflection, I flinched and stumbled away.

'What's with you?' he said.

'Oh, I just don't want to look at myself, always puts me off my dinner.'

He flexed his arms before my mirror. 'You want to go back to body-building,' he said. 'Because after a while you don't notice the pain any more – well, not so much. And you start taking a real pride in your body – like to see how far you can push it. And once you start, really start, you'll never want to stop. 'Cause you always want to go one better. Like, you see my muscles now . . .'

I nodded, even though he wasn't looking at me.

'That's nothing to how they'll be in six months' time,' he smiled at his reflection. 'Now if I ever see a picture of a bloke and a girl on the beach, I always look at the bloke first. It's not that I'm funny,' he added hastily, 'I just like to compare his body with mine.' He continued, smiling away at his reflection, as if he were talking to his greatest friend. 'You want to make something of your body . . .'

Then Steve jerked his head around the door and Tim Grant immediately jumped away from my mirror.

'No hard feelings eh, Grantie?' asked Steve.

'No, no Steve, of course not, it was an epic joke, very clever of you,' said Tim Grant.

He always spoke to Steve in a really creepy way.

'Anyhow,' said Steve, 'now you two have finished would you mind vacating the room because we'd like to use it.'

And Steve proceeded to pull Ash unceremoniously into my bedroom.

She was smiling while clutching on to Steve's hand rather uncertainly, as if she wasn't quite sure what she was holding on to. I couldn't bring myself to speak to her.

Tim Grant exited with a grin and a wink. I followed, unsmiling, blinking away tears of frustration. Still, if this was what Ash wanted . . .

Dowstairs, the first cargo of girls were unloading at the door. I recognised one girl, the rest were more uninviteds. Tim Grant quickly disappeared in their direction. Danny was already 'chatting up' a girl with a shaved head, while leaning on his baseball bat.

I went to close the door when I saw, gliding up the

drive, Anna. I couldn't believe it. What was she doing here?

'Hello, Boffin,' she said.

I squirmed. She was the one person who still got my name wrong. I don't think she did it deliberately – that's what made it worse. Anna aimed a smile at me. Unlike Ash, Anna doesn't waste her smiles. So why was she directing her magnet at me?

I watched her stroll through the hallway, narrowing her eyes at the inferior beings spilling out of the lounge. She deigned to lower her head at one, then returned to me. 'I just came here to wish you every success with your party. It's your first party, isn't it?'

'Yes,' I said, knowing at once she was lying.

'I'm so pleased for you,' she said. 'And it's so noisy already – always a sign of a good party – even if you have to shout to make yourself heard.'

It was noisy – but not so noisy – you had to raise you voice as Anna was starting to do.

'If I might make one suggestion though, Boffin, you must have someone on the door to guard against gate-crashers. Aren't Danny and – Steve about?'

'Danny's in the hallway,' I pointed. Danny's baseball bat was propped up against the wall. He needed both hands now.

'Oh yes,' she added lightly, 'and Steve?'

I stared right at her. 'Steve's upstairs.'

Not one particle of her flinched – to my disappointment.

'That's so like Steve,' she said. 'Well, I'm sorry I can't stay tonight,' she craned forward, nodding at a girl she'd ignored up to now. Her voice continued to rise. 'I can't stay because I have a date. Mark Bateman-Jones. He's eighteen. Just left public school so you wouldn't know him. Might have seen him though, drives a big car, not that I know anything about cars. Still, he's waiting outside now . . .'

I started. I'd heard a door open upstairs. I was sure I had.

Anna beamed another smile around me. 'Anyhow, I really must go. He hates to be kept waiting. Best of luck to you.' She turned away, then turned back again. 'Did you call my name?'

'No,' I said.

'That's funny.'

Then we both heard her name being called. And we both saw Steve leaning over the banisters.

'Oh, hello, Steve,' she called conversationally, 'having a good time?'

'You got a minute?' he said. His voice was anything but conversational.

'No. I haven't, sorry,' she said crisply. 'Goodbye, Boffin.'

'Anna, wait.' Could that be Steve's voice?

She made for the door.

'Anna, please,' he yelped so loudly, those nearby heard and gasped, while Danny moved in, a shocked look on his face.

'I can give you just one minute,' Anna said with awesome indifference before sauntering outside.

Steve tore down those stairs after her, not seeming to notice all the disbelieving stares which followed him. Everyone was muttering about Steve's behaviour – but I could only think of Ash, all alone upstairs.

Ten minutes went by. I mounted the stairs. Ash couldn't be left up there by herself. What could be going through her mind – and heart? But before I got very far Danny tapped me on the shoulder – it was a kind of an official tap, the sort a policeman might give you. And in Steve's absence, I suppose, Danny was in charge.

'Best if we stay out of it,' he said kindly – but firmly.

'But Ash is . . .'

'We'll leave Steve to sort it out. It'll be for the best. If we get involved it'll only make things worse for everyone.' Danny spoke most authoritatively. But was he right? I didn't know. Once again I was up against my deadliest foe: my ignorance.

But anyway, even if I did go up to Ash what could I do? Comfort her with a few more misleading quotes out of books? That's the sum total of all I can offer. So I did nothing save plant myself by the stairs and wait for Ash to come down or Steve to give up.

This was my epic mistake.

The Craziness Goes On and On

They were moving in, surrounding me on all sides. And any second now I'd go under, submerged beneath a tidal wave of white, green, black and pale blue T-shirts.

Every so often I'd smack up against several metres of necklace or my face'd get slapped by a pair of dangly earrings. Mainly though, it was elbows, shoulders and legs. I made contact with so many people that night.

And then Ash swirled downstairs and joined those struggling towards the door. I waved, tried to catch her attention – but only caught someone's armpit. I tried again. But it was hopeless. I was just a metre away from her – and I could have been twenty miles. I was stuck, stranded, marooned in my own party.

My party. That's a laugh. Most of the people here had never seen me before. I began to hate all these invaders, writhing around me. And it became a positive pleasure to poke and push at them, as I tried to pull myself towards

Ash. I craned my head forward. I couldn't see her any more. She must be outside already. Was she going home – or was she seeing Steve – who presumably was still outside with Anna? I had to get outside – fast.

'Hello, Ricky.'

I twisted my neck around to see Katie bobbing past. It was quite a shock meeting someone I'd actually invited.

'This is some party,' she gushed.

The guy with her was smiling too. 'I haven't been to a house-party like this for years,' he said. 'It's a bit like the rush hour on the underground, isn't it?'

I suddenly remembered who he was. That was Memphis, the guy Steve had fought at Ash's party. But tonight he'd been let in, no problem.

'It's all right,' he said. 'Danny and I are mates now.'

I stared at him incredulously. 'It's true, they really are,' cried Katie. 'I wouldn't have brought him if they weren't.'

'It was just a little misunderstanding,' he said. 'That's all.'

Before I could say anything else Katie and Memphis whirled out of sight and I returned to fighting my way out of my own party.

Finally, I landed by the front door. Danny was there and I needed to talk to him about security but he was in a huddle with a girl – I couldn't see if it was the girl he'd been with earlier or not – and anyway, firstly and lastly I wanted to see Ash. I just prayed she hadn't gone home.

Outside I took in a few gulps of fresh air. But the party had even tainted the air outside. There was a faint drizzle and the sky looked low and grey and slimy. While my garden was littered with couples nibbling various parts of each other's anatomy. I glared at them. How dare they all come and lie on my grass – and act as if they were on the beach – or something. I scanned the scene quickly. No sign of Ash – or Anna and Steve.

I collided with a girl in a brightly coloured dress, I murmured, 'Sorry,' without looking at the face. I'd given up looking at faces. But then she said, 'I suppose my brother's on the door.'

'Oh, hello,' I said. It was Danny's sister, Sherrone. Since the pub raid I'd been on a nodding acquaintance with her. She always wore very gaudy clothes but they suited her; she was very attractive.

'Yes, Danny's on the door,' I said, but I couldn't help adding bitterly, 'Not that it matters. He's letting everyone in.'

'He won't let me in,' she said. 'It's all right for him to go out and have a laugh but not me. I'm supposed to just sit in the front room every evening with my mum and that's so boring . . .'

I felt a surge of sympathy for her. 'You go on in if you want,' I said. And if Danny says anything, say I invited you.'

'Well, aren't you lovely?' she replied. She smiled at me excitedly.

'I don't suppose you've seen Ash?' I asked.

'She'll be with Steve, won't she? Danny said . . .'

'Yes, yes,' I said quickly. 'I expect she will.'

She moved away, then turned back. 'Thanks again. I never realised you knew so many people.'

'Neither did I.'

I watched her join the clamour around my front door. Would she enjoy it in there? Perhaps she would. Perhaps you can enjoy all this bundling and hassle if it's not occurring in your own house.

I walked down my drive. A small cluster of neighbours were standing opposite, watching – incredulously no doubt – the goings-on in my house. I put my head down. I didn't want to talk to them, to have to explain what I didn't understand myself. I noticed people bounding in and out of the back gate. Could Ash be in the back garden with Steve – and Anna? Well, certainly I couldn't imagine all three of them together. But then surely Anna must have gone by now. I'd just sneak a look and see if Steve and Ash were there together. If they were I'd sneak away again.

My eyes strayed for a moment and then I saw an extraordinary sight: for hurled out of my front door was Mouse. He fell on to the grass as if he'd just been struck by a high-velocity bullet. I ran over to him.

'Mouse, are you all right?'

Mouse wobbled to his feet, swayed uncertainly, then keeled over again. 'I seem to have temporarily lost the use of my legs,' he said as he eased himself into a sitting position. I joined him on the grass.

'But, Mouse, I had no idea you were in there. I knew you said you'd come tonight but I never actually . . . Oh, look at your suit.'

His frog-green suit was all dishevelled and creased and a look of terror still haunted his face. Only Mouse's voice remained uncrumpled.

'I thought I would never be able to get out . . .'

'Mouse, I'm so sorry. If I'd known the party was going to be like this I'd never have invited you. And I know how much coming here tonight must have cost you – a true act of friendship.'

Mouse lowered his head, and started pulling at the grass. 'It was nothing of the sort; rather it was a demonstration that even I have a vulnerable spot. My visit tonight was prompted by nothing more than a feeling that I might be missing out.' He suddenly peered at me. 'Your words had more of an impact on me than you realised. So much impact in fact, that tonight I found myself donning my only suit, locating your house – despite your garbled directions – and experiencing an emotion which I can only describe as excited anticipation.'

'And now you're disappointed?'

'My primary disappointment,' said Mouse pulling up grass at a furious rate 'is with myself. I pride myself on being an individual. I know that nothing exists outside oneself and I've always loathed the idea that everyone has to be part of a team. But yet tonight, I voluntarily spend time with a group of morons whose idea of a good time is to re-create the Black Hole of Calcutta.' A shudder overtook his whole body. 'After tonight's experience hell can only be an anti-climax.'

I tried to smile. 'Mouse, it's not normally like this, it's just tonight everything's – strange.'

A couple thumped themselves down a few centimetres away from us. We watched the guy take what looked like a pizza out of his mouth, place it on the grass beside him and then dive on to the girl's lips. Mouse started sneezing loudly as if he were allergic to the scene.

'I think it's time I left,' he sniffed.

'Mouse, stay a little longer, at least. We'll go round the back and . . .'

Mouse shook his head. 'I've seen enough. For now I have the proof of something I've long suspected. I was born in the wrong century. In the eighteenth century I could have been the most sociable of men, sitting at Dr Johnson's table and perhaps even inspiring my own Boswell.' He sighed reminiscently as if he were describing scenes which had actually occurred. 'But I can play no part in the mind-frying circus in there. So until the second age of reason dawns which, if history repeats itself, will be during my lifetime, I shall return to the most stimulating companion I know.' He tapped his head. Then he smiled at me kindly. 'I do thank you for inviting me tonight. The experience of being invited somewhere was one I found oddly satisfying.' He pulled his collar up. 'And now I must go home.'

At that moment a convoy of motorbikes started exploding down the road and towards my house. Mouse nodded towards the motorbikes, as they unloaded.

'Look out for yourself,' he said before scurrying away.

I couldn't blame Mouse for going home. I wished I could go with him, especially when I watched these hulks dismounting from their motorbikes. I hadn't seen any of them before – but no doubt they'd soon be rampaging around my house. In fact they only reached the drive, for striding towards them came a reception committee, headed by Steve and Danny.

Steve saw me and patted my head, as he'd patted Ash's earlier. 'Don't worry, Ricky,' he said. 'There's no way those greasy herberts are getting in.'

'Is Ash with . . .' I began, but he'd already marched away. Soon half the party were marching behind him. Some of the girls were outside too, but not Ash. Just about every one of our neighbours was standing outside now. I wondered idly which one of them would be the first to tell Mum about the party.

I've been so stupid, so totally stupid. Did I really think I could give a party without Mum finding out? This evening was so many lunar distances away from what I'd planned, that right now I could only look on in a kind of numb bewilderment.

I turned away to see Anna standing by the back gate, spraying into her mouth something which looked like my breath on a really cold morning. She saw me and to my surprise stepped gingerly around the battle and towards me. I was of course well away from the main line of fire.

And when Anna saw me she said – and this was to prove another of her unforgettable quotes, 'I'm worried about Ash.'

I stared at her incredulously. She was worried about Ash. Well, that was the biggest laugh of the evening. She ruins Ash's evening with her silly play-acting and then says . . .

'Why are you still here?' I said rudely.

'Because I can't leave Ash like . . .'

At that moment a huge cheer erupted. The Greasy Herberts were scrambling on to their motorbikes. Danny and the rest of my party started leaping about, cheering. They had in fact out-numbered the greasy bikers by ten to one.

Danny bounded over to us. 'We saw 'em off for you.'

'Thanks,' I said flatly.

'Nothing like a bit of aggro for getting a party going,' he said. 'It'll be really spinning in there now.'

'That's what I'm afraid of,' I said sourly.

Danny picked up that I was not happy.

'Don't you worry, mate, they're all good blokes in there. We wouldn't let in any trouble-makers and Steve and I aren't leaving until we've cleared up every little thing – are we, Steve?'

Steve joined us, wiping his forehead. He was sweating like a pig. 'Of course not. Going well, isn't it? All right, Anna?'

'I've just been telling Boffin about Ash.' There was a

definite 'I'm really worried about her' snap in her voice.

'Ash's all right,' said Danny quickly.

'Where is she?' I asked Anna.

'In the back garden. She . . .' Steve and Danny had already started edging away, 'See you both inside,' said Steve. 'It's going to bucket down any minute, so I wouldn't hang around outside long.'

They retreated from us while Anna watched them scornfully. 'Look at them!' Then her tone softened, 'I've been trying to speak to Ash – to explain things to her – but she's just sitting as if she's in a trance or something – you'd think she can't see me or hear me . . .' Anna sounded genuinely concerned – and frightened.

I began to feel frightened too.

'Will you talk to her?' asked Anna, 'I know she talks to you.'

'Yes, of course,' I said. 'Let's go now.'

We rushed through the crowds, most of whom were piling inside my house. It was starting to rain quite heavily and the neighbours were watching from their windows now. One called out, 'Richard' really loudly, but I pretended not to hear. I had to get to Ash.

There was no need to push open my gate, it was hanging off its hinges. The lounge door swung open too while people splashed in and out, jostling and shouting at each other. But the garden itself was deserted except for . . .

'See, there she is,' whispered Anna. 'She's been sitting like that for ages.' She started calling out, 'Ash, Ash!'

But the figure sprawled out over the grass never stirred.

'See, she won't answer, it's really spooky.'

Ash was lying right up the top of the garden, underneath our apple trees. Last weekend Mum and I had stood under those very branches, while Dad excitedly pointed out the year's first buds. I have never expected to see Ash underneath those same buds.

I rushed up to her and said her name just once. Instantly she sat up, showing the lovely curve of her breasts. 'Hello, babe,' she said, smiling at me in a way that knifed my heart. It was such a pale, lifeless smile, the smile of someone who's dying inside. I knelt beside her.

Anna hovering above us said, 'Ash, I just want to . . .' At once Ash flinched as if Anna had struck her – and dipped her eyes on to me.

'Why won't you talk to me?' said Anna.

On receiving no answer she pressed on. 'You might at least let me explain, Ash, you can at least do that.'

The rain was getting heavy now, dripping down our faces, our necks, everywhere. But Ash just continued to gaze into the wet darkness, until I felt her hand stroking mine. 'Make her go away,' she said. She sounded like a little girl asking her daddy to get rid of the monster under her bed.

'Perhaps, Anna,' I said, 'it would be better if you left.'

Instead Anna leapt down near us – although her spot was rather more sheltered than ours – and said, 'I'm not going, Ash, until you listen to what I have to say. And if I have to stay out here all night with you, I will,' she added, dabbing her eyes with a tissue. Behind her there were squeals as my guests pushed each other out of the lounge and into the puddles.

Normally at this time the lounge would be curtained up, and soundless, save for Mum stirring the cocoa and Dad snoring in his chair. And I'd be tucked up in bed, my television on low . . . not out here trying to decide if I should tell Anna to 'Get lost and leave Ash alone.' I wanted to – in a way – but there was a note of concern in Anna's voice which prevented me. It was clearly important to Anna that Ash understood what had really happened tonight.

Anna's voice was low and confiding. 'Ash, please listen. This is the truth now, I swear it. Tonight Steve begged me to take him back.' Ash continued to stare into space, but her eyes were blazing with pain as she whispered to me, 'That's a lie.'

Anna leant forward, gripping her black hand-bag with both hands, 'I'm sorry, Ash, it is the truth. But I haven't said yes to Steve.'

'You will though, won't you?' I said bitterly, easing myself closer to Ash, allying myself with her.

'No, I won't. Ash can have Steve if she wants him.'

For the first time Ash stared directly at Anna, her face brimming with disbelief while I said, 'You mean you don't want to go out with Steve any more?' I spoke really slowly as if I were interpreting Anna's words for Ash.

'It's no big deal,' said Anna airily.

I couldn't accept that. 'You came round here tonight to claim Steve back,' I said angrily. 'And don't deny it.

All that about coming round to wish me luck was a load of rubbish, you can't even get my name right.'

For a moment Anna didn't answer. She was visibly shocked by my outburst. Then she said briskly, 'I did come to your party to see Steve – you're right there – but not for the reason you think.' She paused for a moment – 'Steve's blabbed it around school that he's the first guy to ever chuck me. And that's a total lie. Tonight the whole party knows that. They saw Steve run after me and when we were outside he begged me to go out with him. But Ash, I won't.'

'Can't you shut up?' shouted Ash so suddenly, Anna and I both jumped.

Anna bristled. 'Look, I'm not going to start bitching with you. Blokes love it when we do that – that means they've won.'

'Won? This is not a game,' cried Ash.

'Yes it is, Ash,' said Anna. 'And if we don't use them, they'll use us.' Anna's voice softened. 'I'm sorry about tonight. I never meant to hurt you, that's the truth. And hate me if you must, Ash, but hate Steve too. He's the one who left you upstairs tonight and hasn't bothered to see you since.'

For a moment Ash said nothing. Then she got shakily to her feet. Anna stood up too. I thought I'd better get up as well. Anna smiled, displaying a set of fine white teeth. 'Ash, let's be friends again – please.'

Ash let out a choking noise, which sounded like a strangled laugh but was actually the first blast of her pain before it exploded into words, 'You bitch,' she screamed. 'You absolute bitch, you've ruined my life!' The words became muffled as tears streamed down Ash's face.

'Oh, Ash, shout at me but don't cry, I can't bear that.' Anna gave a kind of half laugh. 'Crying puts lines on your face. Ash, please stop.' But I don't think Ash could stop now. She put her hand out to me, I gripped it hard.

It was at this moment Danny came sauntering over to us – he was carrying an umbrella – which I recognised as one of ours. 'Hello, you lot. What are you all doing standing out here in the rain?' he asked, all cool and easy.

Anna groaned. I felt like groaning too. Danny must have known what we were doing here. But Danny continued the play-acting by saying to me, hyper-casually, 'It's really hotting up in there. We're keeping an eye on things for you, so don't worry about that.'

'Thank you so much,' I said dryly. 'My back gate's broken by the way.'

Danny gave me a puzzled look. 'Steve'll repair that for you, no sweat. We'll see you straight, Ricky, no fear. Anyway,' he smiled, embarrassed, 'the reason I'm out here talking in the rain is I'm acting as a kind of messenger from Steve to Anna. Er, Steve'd like a word with Anna. When you're ready,' he added.

Anna's voice assumed an icy overtone. 'Well, why can't Steve come out here?' Danny cringed. 'Out here? Out here now? Is that wise? I mean,' he laughed nervously, 'it's a bit wet, isn't it?'

Anna was about to reply when Ash sprang towards her, glaring furiously as if she was about to hit her. 'I don't want Steve out here and I don't want you. I just want to be left alone. Can't you understand that?' She turned to me, 'Make them go away, Ricky.'

I drew her up against me. I could feel the turmoil going on inside her. Anna might mean well – but she was just hurting Ash. So I said quietly, 'I think it would be better if you both went inside – for now.'

Danny didn't need telling twice. But Anna trailed after him reluctantly, defeated. Ash and I remained locked in a hug. The rain was starting to turn vicious, battering our faces with millions of tiny cruel blows.

'It's hail-storming, you go in,' said Ash.

'Only if you come too,' I said.

'No, no, I can't go in yet.'

'Then you're stuck with me.'

'But it's your party.'

'No, it's Steve and Danny's party. I feel like a piece of driftwood in there.'

Ash clutched me tightly. 'But that's how I feel.'

'We're just two pieces of driftwood floating down the stream of life and going nowhere,' I said, wondering if I'd actually made that up myself.

'I like it when you talk like that,' Ash sighed as if I were telling her a bedtime story. 'Talk some more.'

'Well, I . . .' I looked up at the apple trees heavy with rain, as they swayed and dripped about us. 'If you look up there,' I said, 'you can see some little buds. My dad showed me them. He always gets really excited about them, says they're the first sign that winter's over.'

'Oh, where? Where are they?' cried Ash excitedly.

'Up there, see,' I pointed them out.

'No, no, I can't.'

'They're right in front of you, they look like swellings.'

Ash giggled. 'That sounds rude. No, I can't see them. I can't see anything tonight, I'm all woozy.' Her voice became sharp with pain again. 'The nerve of that girl coming out here telling me those lies. She's so full of tricks and games, no wonder Steve's all mixed up.'

'Well, I wouldn't . . .' I faltered.

'And that's why, dear Ricky, I'm going to ask you, ask you to do me one last favour. Will you, please?'

By now my heart was thumping so loudly against my chest I felt for sure it would break away from me and into its real home, with Ash.

'I'll do anything you want,' I said fervently. She kissed me, a glimmer of warmth against the icy lashing my face was taking from the rain.

'Ask Steve to come out here,' she whispered.

'But he won't come out here,' I cried, stunned she should even suggest such a thing. She stared at me, hurt flickering across her face. 'Yes, he will. Oh Ricky, please help me. I know if you get Steve out here I can sort this out.'

'But, Ash, don't you understand? Steve was using you tonight,' I went on as gently as I could. 'You've got to face it. Steve doesn't care for you as we thought.'

'No, no,' Ash started shaking her head and putting her hands up to her ears.

'Ash, he's not worthy of you,' I shouted, 'Anna was right.'

'So she's turned you against me too, has she?' cried Ash. 'Well, go away. I don't need you either. If you won't help me, I'll get Steve myself.' And before I knew it she was out of my hands and running towards the lounge.

'Ash, wait, wait,' I yelled, puffing after her, my shoes squelching over the muddy grass. But I was too late. The most awful event of the night had begun. Ash was hammering on the lounge window, shrieking, 'Steve, Steve, come out here, just for a minute.'

I hung behind her, whispering, 'Ash, don't degrade yourself like this.' But I knew I could no more stop Ash than I could hold back a thunderstorm.

'Steve, Steve, its's me!' she cried.

The party inside gazed in wonderment at this bewitching novelty. There was loud laughter and excited babblings of 'Who is it?' and they gathered around the window trying to identify the dishevelled figure beating on the glass even harder than the rain.

I don't think anyone recognised Ash at first. For the black mascara had run all down her face making her look strange and eerie, almost like a ghost. 'Steve, please . . .' Ash's voice was ebbing away, her rose-coloured nails sliding down the glass.

And where was Steve? He was there in the lounge and it was easy to pick him out – he and Danny were the only ones not by the window. They were crouched in the corner, neither acknowledging they knew the girl beating on the window.

'Clear off,' yelled a voice at Ash. Foam was aimed at the window, but there were words of sympathy too, for the phantom – who wailed, 'Steve' once more before tumbling away from the window and towards me.

I gazed at my Ash, now so small, pathetic, and hopeless. I touched her. I couldn't feel any limbs, only water. It was as if she was dissolving away – and all for Steve. I could have given her so much but she didn't want me. Only Steve. A spasm of anger uncoiled inside me. 'Are you satisfied now?' I spat the words at her.

She didn't reply, just ran like the wind out of my house, down the road and away. I puffed after her, shouting apologies but she'd gone, disappeared, turned to air.

I walked back to the party, racked with guilt. She must have run home. Perhaps though it was for the best for there was no way she could walk back into the party after . . . not after . . . I'll never forget the way she'd wailed out Steve's name and the way she'd looked – as if all the life had been knocked out of her. Shivers went up and down my spine and I must admit they were still angry shivers. Why is it Steve she loves? Why not me?

Steve and Danny were slouched by the lounge door when I returned. The rain was easing off and there was a small knot of people outside examining a smear of red lipstick on the window – it was as if they were poring over Ash's blood.

I shouted at Steve, 'She's gone. Why wouldn't you come out?'

Danny immediately moved in front of Steve as if he were his bodyguard.

'Steve didn't go out because she was as drunk as a skunk and didn't know what she was doing,' he said quickly.

'She never could hold a drink,' muttered Steve.

'But that's rubbish . . .' I began.

'Let's cool it,' said Danny. 'Ricky, you'd better come in and dry off. You're soaked to the skin and we can't have that.' His voice was low and reassuring but he was warning me off. As far as he and Steve were concerned the subject was closed. I followed them inside to the lounge.

Steve thrust a can in my hand. 'This'll warm you up,' he said. His hand was shaking slightly and he looked as if someone had poured a bucket of sweat over him but his smile was as feverish as ever. I wondered what was going on inside him. He must be sorry and ashamed really.

'Catch you later,' Steve said, disappearing with Danny.

To my surprise Anna was still at the party, sitting on the settee, a glass of wine in her hand, a score of admirers at her feet. We spoke briefly about Ash and she didn't try and hide how badly she felt about the whole thing. Then I wandered like a sleepwalker through a lounge, thick with smoke, music and the smell of BO. I recognised the music, liked it, but tonight it just stoked up feelings of emptiness. I couldn't stay in the room. I felt as if all my senses were being blocked up.

I staggered out of the lounge, through the crowds jammed in the hallway and into the kitchen. In here even the floor was sweating – there were great pools of something on the floor anyway.

I just wanted to go home. This wasn't my home.

Tonight, Steve and Danny had transformed my boringly safe home into a place where crazy things rushed up at you and the craziness went on and on. That was what terrified me. I couldn't see where tonight's craziness would end, it seemed to have no end.

But actually the party finished sooner than I'd dared hope. One of my guests had started firing a barrage of plant pots into next door's garden. This assault of flying plant pots led my neighbours to call the police.

The police arrived ten minutes later and when they saw there were no adults about, they closed the party and started searching for drugs.

'We don't take drugs,' said Steve very indignantly. He took charge. The police assumed it was his house. Much hassle followed but I was largely unaware of it. I had another problem of my own. I couldn't catch my breath. I went through the coughing, wheezing, gasping routine that makes up one of my asthmatic attacks. Well, if I was going to breathe my last I didn't want it to be in public. So I slipped up to my bedroom and shuffled about for my inhaler. Then I just lay back on my mattress – I didn't switch the light on. I could smell how unfamiliar my bedroom was – I didn't need to see it too. And the darkness was so cool and soothing. I meant to just lie there for a minute before ringing Ash.

I awoke to the sound of hoovering – a sound I often awoke to at the weekends as Mum cleaned up after the excesses of our Friday or Saturday nights. But it wasn't Mum downstairs. Was it?

It was Danny hoovering the lounge while his sister, Sherrone, rather absent-mindedly wiped the windows.

When he saw me, Danny switched off the hoover. 'I looked in on you upstairs,' he said. 'Been sleeping it off, have you?' He grinned.

'Yes, I must have dozed off.'

'You breathe really heavily when you sleep, don't you?' said Danny. He didn't say it unkindly, so I just smiled, while looking around me in some bewilderment.

'Has everyone gone?' I asked.

'Everyone,' said Danny, 'not even anyone hiding under the settee. We've checked. No, the pigs cleared the place really quickly. A pity, when it was going so well, but it often happens that way.'

Sherrone peered through the lounge window, 'They're still out there.'

'Who's out there?' I asked.

'Just Steve and Anna,' said Danny. 'I'll get them to come in in a minute to lend a hand.' He turned to Sherrone, 'Now Ricky's awake you can go upstairs and clean your teeth, don't mind, do you, Ricky?'

'Well no, but why?' I murmured bewilderedly.

Sherrone giggled. 'It's to take away the smell of alcohol so my dad doesn't know I've been drinking. Though he might wonder why I've come home from Cathy's reeking of toothpaste.'

'Go on, get upstairs,' said Danny. 'No arguments.'

'Watches over me like a mother hen,' said Sherrone, 'doesn't let any boy come near me . . . he's a right case my brother,' she added affectionately, before leaving to clean her teeth.

Danny shook his head, 'She takes some watching.' He sounded more like her father than her brother.

'Is Tim Grant about?' I asked suddenly. I couldn't imagine him leaving without Steve and Danny.

'Ah well,' Danny looked uncomfortable. His manner suggested he was about to tell me some very sad news. 'Grantie took a girl upstairs and, shall we say, couldn't rise to the occasion.'

'But how do you know?'

Danny shook his head and looked grim, 'These things get about.'

I decided the first time I did it – whatever century that was – it definitely wouldn't be at a party.

'Anyway, better get on,' he said. 'Steve and I promised we'd clear up for you – and we're men of our word.'

'I'm going to ring Ash,' I said.

Danny started but then replied, 'Yeah, you do that.' And just as I was opening the door he said, 'Tonight's been a real downer for Steve. He thinks Anna humiliated him. Ash couldn't have picked a worse time.' Then before I could answer he resumed his hoovering.

To the accompaniment of Danny's hoovering I rang Ash.

'Hello, is Ash there, please?' I croaked. Perhaps Ash didn't want to speak to me.

An unfamiliar female voice said, 'Well, she is – but she's in bed asleep. She came back drenched from a party, had a bath and went straight to bed. I need to talk to her myself – there's a bit of a family crisis here. I'm Jo, her sister, by the way. You're not Steve Almond are you?'

'No, I'm . . . no-one important,' I slapped the phone down. Anna was hovering by the kitchen door, Steve beside her. 'You just rang Ash?' she asked.

'Yes, she's in bed asleep. I spoke to her sister Jo. She said something about a family crisis.'

'If Jo's there, she's the family crisis,' said Anna sharply.

'She's a right scrubber,' muttered Steve. He looked pale and tired. 'You say Ash's asleep?'

'Yes.'

'Best place for her, she was way out of order tonight,' he said gruffly before advancing uncertainly out of the kitchen. 'I'll see how wrecked it is upstairs.' He looked pretty wrecked himself.

After he left Anna said, 'Steve asked me out again. I said no.'

'Because of Ash?'

'Because I don't fancy him any more,' said Anna matter-of-factly. 'It often happens that way, I'm mad about

212

a bloke for a while and then one day I see him and I don't fancy him any more. I used to be really ashamed about it – but not any more,' she started fumbling about in her bag. 'Excuse me doing this,' she said, as she flung her left arm up in the air and started rubbing her roll-on underneath it. 'I'm not a sweating kind of person,' she said, rubbing under her right arm, 'but tonight . . . and I hate sweaty smells on myself.' Then she put the roll-on away and started talking about smells and how to get rid of those in the kitchen until she suddenly asked – 'Does Ash hate me?'

'Well, tonight she said things – but later . . .'

'Mmm, mmm,' Anna turned away and started fiddling in her bag as she said, more to herself than me, 'When I had my appendix out and I was ill for weeks afterwards, only one person came to see me every day – Ashley. Oh, the first couple of days everyone piled round my house but they soon got bored of visiting and I don't blame them – I'd have been just the same. I hate being near sick people. But Ash, she came round every single day, some-times just for a few minutes but every day I knew she'd be there. And that was good. I had one friend I could rely on. And now she hates me. Ah well, I tried to explain.' She shrugged her shoulders, 'That's it, I suppose.' She started piling up the plates on the kitchen table. 'We'd better get on, there's masses to clear up in here. I'll wash if you wipe. Okay?'

We worked in silence. Anna, like me, seemed lost in thought until she opened the cooker and said, 'There's a plate of shrivelled-up chicken, chips and baked beans in here.'

'And if you look under the baked beans,' I said, 'you'll find some greens too, probably cabbage.'

Anna forked under the beans. 'Why yes, you're right.'

'Mum always hides them there. I leave my greens, you see, that was tonight's dinner.'

'What's your mum like?' asked Anna.

I rubbed a hand over my face. I couldn't bring myself to describe her, I just said, 'My mum's about to get the biggest shock of her life. She won't believe what's happened here tonight – she won't believe it.'

Steve, Danny and Anna did their valiant best at clearing up. I must give them that. But even after a typical Friday night, Mum's eagle eyes can sight great boulders of dust next morning. So what would she make of all the stains, burn-marks, breakages, strange smells?

Steve and Danny knew I was worried and Danny kept trying to cheer me up by telling me stories of parties where even the telephone had been stolen and generally saying how it could have been a lot worse. Steve said very little, he didn't look at all well actually and when he left with Danny and Anna – Sherrone had been taken home by Danny much earlier – he was leaning on Danny as if he couldn't even walk without his support.

As I closed the door on them, deep, deep depression set in. I pottered around, trying to cover up some more of the stains – but just kept finding fresh ones. Tomorrow's going to be a day of mighty hassle – no avoiding that – while

214

tonight . . . I'd hated every minute of tonight. In the end I couldn't bear looking at the mess that was my party any longer – and I crashed out upstairs.

Steve had put the blankets back on my bed – but not properly – and I had this dry bitter taste in my mouth which I couldn't get rid of . . . I didn't expect to fall asleep for hours. But instead, I fell asleep almost at once. Soon I was dreaming. I was on a bus and Ash was tapping on the windows, shouting at me to 'Get out'. I ran to the exit but I couldn't open the door and behind me I heard all this laughing from the passengers. And all of a sudden I recognised the faces: they were the people on the bus that had crashed.

'But aren't some of you dead?' I cried.

'We're all dead – but we've just come back for you. We missed you.'

'No, no,' I yelled and I started hammering at the door and calling out for Ash to help me – but suddenly I couldn't breathe. I was gasping for breath and I could hear them cackling behind me.

I woke up, gasping. It's all right, just a dream, I said to myself, just a dream. Calm down. I'm here, safe in my bedroom. I opened my eyes. But no, this isn't my bedroom. Where am I?

Black Snow

I can't see. I can't do anything except cough. I don't even know if I'm really awake. And it's as if my mind's gone away for a minute while I lie here, suspended between . . . is it possible to dream and still be awake? And why don't I recognise this place?

Suddenly my mind checks back in, a little of the confusion falls away. I must be in my bedroom. Where else can I be? Only for some reason my bedroom's filling up with smoke.

I've got to get out of here, fast.

I stumble out of my bed. I can't see anything except smoke – which is pouring into my mouth – gaining a stranglehold on my neck. I'm choking hard and groping for the door. At last I touch something other than smoke. I touch a wall. I start tapping furiously, the door must be near here. But all I hit against are walls – no door.

Now I'm lunging around the room, banging on all the

walls like a maniac. I hear myself whimpering – between gasps – because I'm trapped. There is no door, no way out, and I don't know what to do.

I'm scraping at the walls now, when something falls on to my hands. I scrunch it in my hand and laugh. It's a poster. I must be in my bedroom. There must be a door. Seconds later I fall on to a sharp and metallic object. I'm so weak now I can hardly turn the door handle. But I'm out.

I fall on to the landing, coughing and spitting while my breathing sounds like it's been played at the wrong end. I can't stop breathing at this furious rate for ages.

Billowing over me are fumes and smoke. My door isn't closed. I stand by the door. My room seems so small now, yet when I was running around in there I swear it was the size of Wembley Stadium. The smoke parts slightly, almost deferentially, before its source. Flames have landed on my curtains. They won't stop at my curtains either. They would devour this whole house if they could. I've got to go back in there and stop them. Don't be silly; that's risky, foolhardy.

I start coughing again. I stand away from the door. There's no way I'm going back in there. But then again, if I don't, the fire will surely spread. And Mum will find out! I tear back into my bedroom. I have a plan. But I've got to be quick. With shaking hands I whip the blanket off my bed and hurl it over my curtains. With one throw the fire is smothered, wiped out.

The smoke still clusters about but at least I've shut up

its supplier. I must close the bedroom door now to prevent any more smoke creeping downstairs. I steal one final triumphant glance at the blanket. But my victory is short-lived. Round the side of the blanket are a few little flames, they're unsmothered and raring to go.

Panicking like mad I rip down to the kitchen and find our yellow bucket. Every room I run through is clogged with smoke now. This adds to my fear that somehow this fire is going to overtake me. At least the bucket is where we always leave it. I fill it right to the brim with water, then bound up the stairs, not noticing how much water I slop on the way.

Inside my bedroom the blanket is ablaze, red-hot. I tip water all over the blanket – at once there's a really vicious sizzling noise, as if the fire is spitting with rage at being extinguished. But now the fire is wiped out, isn't it?

There's still the smoke everywhere but hopefully that will start ebbing away and have disappeared completely before my parents get home. I start to look at my watch. I never quite make it. There's no need. I hear a key in the door, a scream, and two people padding up the stairs.

They fall into my bedroom.

'I've just been putting a fire out,' I say.

For a moment they stare at me, disbelievingly. They look petrified. Then they rush towards me. I expect anger, shouting, instead I'm engulfed in their arms, pulled outside and I only hear cries of relief.

'Thank God,' says my mum, wrapping herself around me. 'Oh, thank God.' A few tears escape down her face.

Dad is trembling too and trying to steady his voice. 'You're sure you're all right, boy?' He pats my arms as if to check they're not about to fall off.

'Yes, I'm all right. I just woke up and there was this fire in my room. I didn't know what was going on at first.'

'Thank God you woke up,' says Mum. 'Oh, thank God,' She sounds as if she is about to sing a gospel song but She settles for smothering me beneath her genuine imitation fur coat.

Dad says gravely, 'Tell us exactly what happened, son.'

Mum releases me from her furry grip and I, feeling faintly ridiculous at holding forth on the landing in only my pyjamas, narrate, 'I woke up to find all this smoke around me. I couldn't see anything, couldn't even find the door for ages.'

'Could you get your breath all right?' asks Mum. 'It didn't bring on your . . .'

'No, no,' I say quickly, frightened that just hearing the word asthma might set off another attack. So instead I say, 'I went back into my room to put the fire out. I thought it the best thing to do,' I add with a cringing attempt at modesty.

But Mum and Dad stare at me aghast. 'You went back in?' cries Dad. 'But don't you realise how dangerous and foolish that was? Why did you do it?' Mainly so Mum didn't find out but I couldn't say that? Instead I reply simply, 'I wanted to stop the fire spreading.'

'Your first priority must always be your own safety,' says Dad.

'You could have suffocated to death in there,' cries Mum and both she and Dad do a kind of collective shiver.

'You must never do that again.' Dad is almost shouting, I've never seen him so worked up. I agree with him, though.

'I think the fumes must have sent me a bit stupid,' I say apologetically. This seems to calm Dad down. 'Anyway,' he says, 'we'd best open all the windows.' Mum nods. 'We don't want those fumes on our chests tonight.' She turns to Dad. 'And we won't rest easy in our beds until we know how that fire started. I told you I heard sizzling noises in our bedroom and that I didn't think the wires up here had been earthed properly.'

I realise I haven't yet thought about the cause of the fire. At the time I'd just assumed it was a natural event like a thunderstorm over which I had no control. But something had caused it. I pray Mum is right and it's to do with the wires upstairs. Please don't let it be anything to do with the party.

Mum and I open the windows downstairs.

'I told your father to have those wires and fuses checked, but does he listen? I said one day there's going to be a terrible accident . . .'

I watch her open the lounge windows. Will she notice the remnants of foam left on there? But Mum doesn't notice anything. All the signs of the party are cloaked behind smoke for now. But I must tell Mum and Dad about the party. And I'm going to – any second.

'What a thing for you to wake up to,' says Mum. 'I tell

you, when your father and I opened the door and saw all that smoke, well, I flew up those stairs with my heart in my mouth. How are you feeling now, Nip?'

'Oh, much better.'

'You're still coughing though. I'll get you some of your cough mixture and a nice cup of tea. You'd like that, wouldn't you?' Mum bustles around in the kitchen while I'm quaking on the settee. I'm going to tell her about the party now, for sure.

But she chats on relentlessly. 'I'll be busy tomorrow, there's no mistake. Every curtain in the house will have to be washed, all the paintwork wiped down for that smoke gets everywhere. Then there's your bedroom, well, your carpet will be a write-off . . .' Any second now I'll insert my news about the party and give Mum and Dad their second shock of the night.

'And Kay sends her love.' Mum has changed the subject without me noticing.

I say hastily, 'How is Kay – and Paul?'

'Mother and son both doing very well,' coos Mum. 'He's a dear little soul, just like Kay was at that age, he's even got her toes. Kay was so sorry you couldn't go round tonight but she understood. Did you get all your studying done?'

Now is the moment to tell her. But I let the moment pass. Then Mum sniffs. 'There's such a funny smell in the kitchen, it smells like cheese that's gone off, only we haven't got any cheese.' At the same time Dad is coming down the stairs saying, 'Well, that's very strange.'

'What is?' asks Mum.

'Well, the fire appears to have started on the boy's computer, by the curtains. For the plastic casing's burnt right down, it's all charred . . .' Poor Dad. He sounds so puzzled and keeps saying 'What a mystery it all is.'

Well, Dad, I can solve the mystery for you. One of my dear, uninvited guests may have been in my bedroom messing about by the curtains and left his or her cigarette to stand on my computer. But Dad would never suss that out. It would never even occur to him that I'd have a cigarette in my room. It really wouldn't.

I look at my parents. I don't want to tell them. I don't want their image of me to crumble before my eyes. I just want to say, 'Goodnight,' and curl up into a tight ball and bounce away. But instead, I'm coming clean. I have no choice, now.

'Mum, Dad, please sit down, there's something I've got to tell you.' I sound as if I'm going to tell them of my forthcoming marriage – not about a wild party.

They circle round me. 'What's up, son?' asks Dad.

'There was a party here tonight.'

'Here?' my mum echoes disbelievingly and then she looks around her, while the smoke obligingly starts to clear.

'It was only meant to be a little party but it got out of hand. This house was full of people I didn't know. They messed up things, broke things. I couldn't control it,' I add lamely.

Mum is already sniffing the carpet and on the trail . . .

'Look,' she cries, pointing at the carpet, then she sees how the backs of the chairs have been chipped. . . . She walks around the lounge exclaiming over every object, every corner, just about every inch. Then she continues her inventory of destruction in the kitchen. Dad follows, dazed and confused.

The kettle screams on, unnoticed, while Mum calls out details of the kitchen damage. I go and stand by the lounge window, in the corner. And I feel so ashamed. This is their home, their sanctuary from the world. They love this house. They file silently through the lounge to inspect the damage in the dining room. I dread them returning. When they do Mum asks me, 'Did they go upstairs too?' I nod.

She moans piteously. 'I'd better see what state . . .'

'I've been upstairs,' interrupts Dad. 'It didn't look too bad to me, not as bad as down here anyway. Best thing you can do is sit down for a minute. You've gone as white as a sheet.'

They both sit hunched together on the settee. I hate seeing them like this.

I burst out, 'I'm sorry, so very sorry. This wasn't meant to happen.'

'Why didn't you ask us first?' asks Dad in such a reasonable voice.

I cannot answer him, only hang my head miserably.

Then Mum screams. 'Our house is wrecked, wrecked!'

I want her to go on. I want her to shout like crazy at me. But instead, Dad puts his arm around her and talks to her in a very low, reassuring voice while I stare at the many varieties of stain on the carpet. And no-one speaks. No-one knows what to say. For all three of us have found ourselves catapulted into a scene we've never prepared for. No wonder a look of bewilderment has apparently set on Mum and Dad's faces. They don't know this mad boy before them. They only know their nice, quiet, hard-working boffin of a son. I can almost hear them asking themselves, Where has our son gone?

To my surprise and slight embarrassment, they're holding hands as Dad whispers to Mum, comforting her – just as I'd tried to comfort Ash a few hours earlier – only he's doing a far more expert job than me. I'd give anything not to be here now. I think I'd rather be in prison than in this lounge. And suddenly it's as if I'm not here as Mum starts saying in a low, weary voice, quite unlike her own, 'Where have we gone wrong? We've always considered him. We've never pushed him out of the house like some mothers I could name. I wanted him to look on his home as a bolt-hole from the world. The world may knock him about but there's still his home – where he can feel safe and wanted – always. And yet, as soon as our backs are turned he has the house smashed up by a gang of yobs. We've gone wrong somewhere.'

I can't listen to any more of that. I must make them understand why I held the party. Only I don't have time to organise my thoughts so it all comes out rather garbled. 'Mum, I swear to you I never intended anything to happen to this house. Do you really think I'd want my home to be mutilated? It's been awful for you coming home to – this. But it was pretty bad seeing it happen before my eyes and knowing it's all my fault. I didn't think. That's my trouble – I didn't think. And I wanted people to like me. You see, you two like me – though probably not at the moment – but no-one else does, much, if at all. And recently I thought I'd made some friends and I wanted to please them and show off to them. But it all went wrong.' I pause. Mum and Dad are staring at me so intently, they unnerve me. I continue talking to their shoes. 'And I'll make it up to you. I promise. I'll pay for all the damage when I can,' I add, remembering I've all the food and drink from the party to pay for by working at Bunce's every night, 'and I'll take as long as it takes to clear up. Even if it takes until Christmas, which it won't,' I say hastily.

'You just tell me what to do and I'll do it.' I pause expectantly.

A smile brushes across Dad's face and he says to Mum, 'We can die for them but we can't live for them. We must let them make their own mistakes occasionally.'

Mum nods and slowly sits up. 'Worse things happen at sea,' she says softly. Dad's smile widens and I start breathing a little. 'Tomorrow we'll set the boy to work,' he says. 'With some elbow grease we can clear a lot of this mess up.'

A gleam comes into Mum's eye. You can almost hear the life rushing back into her. 'We'll break the back of it now,' she announces. Dad and I stare at her incredulously – it's half past two in the morning. But Mum doesn't let a little thing like that bother her. 'I've no intention of coming down to this mess in the morning.' She stands up, 'So come on, all hands on deck.'

We work until five o'clock. Weird as it sounds the time goes quickly and in a way it feels good to be doing something. We don't exactly break the back of it – but every room is bathed in sweet, clean, familiar smells. Mum goes from room to room, sniffing appreciatively. They reassure her that normality is being restored. And as the house returns to normal, so does she. Even to making us all our night-time cocoa, although as Dad jokes it should really be early morning tea. While the cocoa ritual takes place I creep up to my room. The one room untouched by Mum's restoring smells.

It would be a shock to see any room so burnt out but when it's your own bedroom it's far worse. My bedroom is now pitch black, the wardrobe, the mirror, the bookcase, everything is covered in sinister black snow. And this snow isn't going to melt away. Look at my room from any corner and you'll just see deep, unending blackness. It's as if I'm sitting in my own tomb. And I could have died tonight. Very easily. Especially if I'd been a Lad and got out of my head, then I certainly would never have woken up.

So once again I cheat death. I escape a bus crash and see it as a sign to stop being a boffin. Now I escape a fire, is that a sign too?

'I expect it all seems like a dream now.' Dad is in the doorway wearing his usual apologetic smile.

Away from my bedroom it's like a dream but here it's all too real. For there on the wall are all my handprints, from when I couldn't find the door. And over there, that poster I ripped.

Dad peers at each thing I point out as if they were exhibits in a museum. He feels awkward, wants to say something but doesn't know what. He picks up a paperback from the floor, 'Ah, *The Big Sleep* by Raymond Chandler. I always meant to read this.' He opens it up, soot gushes out from its pages. He hastily puts the book down again. I go over to my bookshelf. Every time I open a book soot streams out. It seems as if every one of my books is marked by this black plague. And that sight distresses me more than I'd have thought. Many of those books have been unopened for months – but they're still a part of me. 'What a mess,' I say – 'and all my own fault.'

Dad mumbles. 'Taking the odd wrong turning doesn't mean you're going in the wrong direction.' He stares at me. 'When you're young you've got to get out in the world a bit, only natural.' Then immediately he looks away, just like comedians do when they've said something very cheeky. Dad's always been embarrassed about giving me advice. My dad's an easy man to underestimate: he's quite shy and quiet and sleeps a lot. But I remember Dad on the day Kay got married. I'd been in a funny mood all day and when she left for the honeymoon with the geek she'd married and all those silly relatives we hardly ever saw were calling out things, Dad put his arm around my shoulders and said, 'Fancy a walk?'

As we walked through this graveyard Dad told me that seeing Kay in her wedding dress today had brought tears to his eyes and he didn't mind admitting he'd cried, as it was good to let your emotions out occasionally. Then he said to me that if I wanted to have a bit of a cry, to go right ahead, and I said, 'How silly' and cried for an hour.

'Right, you two out of here or you'll be coughing all night and keeping me awake,' Mum bustles in. 'I've made the settee up for you downstairs,' she says to me.

'Oh, I'd have done that,' I say.

'I wanted it done properly,' she replies. She looks around my room, her eyes glistening. 'I've been meaning to sort this room out for ages, never liked that carpet . . .'

So I'm sleeping in the lounge and Mum is fiddling about with my cocoa and I know she is building up to a lecture and unlike Dad, Mum delivers her lectures loudly and clearly. Sure enough, when I'm propped up on the couch she says, 'Next time something like this happens . . .'

'There won't be a next time,' I interrupt.

'Next time something like this happens,' repeats Mum, 'tell your father and me straight away. Don't wait for us to find out. I can cope with anything if I'm told.'

'All right, Mum, I will. Even though I might be doing things that – that seem a bit strange to you sometimes.'

'Just remember, son,' she says, 'we might shout at you and call you all the names under the sun but no matter what you've done, even if you've . . .' Mum paused for a suitable example, 'even if you've murdered someone –

we'll always be there in your corner. Will you remember that?'

'Yes, Mum.'

'And don't forget to wash that mug up when you've finished. If there's one thing I hate first thing in the morning, it's being faced with dirty mugs.' Only Mum with a mountain of destruction around her could worry about the fate of my mug.

I nod. 'And Mum, I really am sorry about . . .'

Mum shakes away my apology. 'No, you're a good boy really. I know that. Now don't sit up too long, you're looking tired.'

As it was now half past five in the morning that wasn't altogether surprising. But then Mum has thought I've looked tired every day of my life. I'd been dreading telling Dad – and Mum about tonight. Yet, they've coped and I'm amazed at how well they've coped. I'd never realised before quite what a strong team they are.

I try and sleep on the settee but I can't. Basically I'm too fat for settees, and I find it hard to sleep when half my back is lying over the side.

I sit up. Here I am, a refugee from my own bedroom. In a way though, I've always felt like a refugee. The world's always belonged to other people – not me. I've spent my life either pleasing people – or dodging them. And for fifteen years I handed my life over to Mum, my teachers, my elders. I lived on their approval; their wish was my command. Then I break free, decide to be the real me and promptly hand my life over to Steve. For that's what I've done, isn't it? And if my party really was Steve's party, whose fault is that? I gave the party to please him, to keep in with him. And my main ambition these last few weeks has been to become Steve's clone. Only tonight I saw Steve doing things I never want to do. Like the way he used Ash – and left her outside – that was cruel. If it had been me Ash loved I would have – well, there's no sense in thinking about that.

So what do I do now? Did Ricky die in the fire tonight? If so, where does that leave me? For if I'm not Boffin or Ricky – who am I?

Ash's Gone

'Rich, what sort of name is that?' Steve's voice crackled disbelievingly down the phone.

'Well, I just got a bit tired of Ricky,' I said. 'So I've decided to call myself Rich from now on, you're the first to know.' I couldn't tell Steve that every time I heard the name Ricky I thought of a disastrous party, a burnt-out bedroom and deep, unending blackness – Rich was my fresh start.

'It sounds a bit funny to me, still, if that's what you want. Anyway, Rich, are you coming down Penn Fair tonight?'

'Can't. I haven't got any money, not a penny. I have to save up to weigh myself.'

'I'll pay for you. I'm well loaded tonight. And I owe you one after last Friday.'

'Well, that's very generous of you.'

I considered. I wasn't a great one for fairs. On the other

hand I've got out of the habit of spending Friday nights at home and the thought of a whole evening just sitting in with my parents – much as I loved them – filled me with dread.

'Yeah, all right I'll go. I suppose everyone's going.' I was thinking of Ash.

'Reckon so. Danny-boy can't go, he's gone to Birmingham with his waxworks for the weekend, the pegleg.'

'What about Tim Grant? Is he better now?'

This morning right in the middle of assembly Tim Grant had had a kind of fit. It was really disturbing to see him suddenly unable to control his own body and just thrashing about the room. It took three teachers to get him outside. For the first time ever there was total silence in that hall for the rest of assembly.

He was taken home and I knew Steve was going round to see him straight after school. But when Steve spoke of Tim Grant now there was indignation – not pity in his voice.

'Would you believe it, I go round his house and I'm practically assaulted by his old dear. I can't get any sense out of her at first, then I find out what's bugging her, she only thinks I've been giving Grantie steroids.'

'Why should she think that?'

''Cause it came out today that Grantie's been taking steroids. Anyway, when his old dear susses that I don't know anything about these steroids she lets me see him. And as soon as he sees me, he starts blubbering away. Tells me he's been pumping himself with these steroids for ages. I said to him, "That's why you've been falling down on the job. That stuff makes you sterile, you know."'

'Does it?' I said vaguely. 'But in assembly today was it the steroids that made him . . .?'

'Couldn't tell you. His mum thinks it was. I tell you she was like a crazy woman herself when she saw me. She even forgot to put on her posh accent at first. Anyway I told Grantie what a total nut-job he's been.'

'Poor old Grantie,' I said.

'I thought you'd be pleased, you hate him.'

'I used to hate him. Unfortunately I also understand him all too well.' I thought of him on the night of my party – just one week ago – gloating in my mirror at his new body the way somebody else might gloat over a new car. He'd given his body over to an image and the more his muscular physique was admired, the more steroids he had to push down himself. Until today when his body finally freaked out – exploded. Oh yes, I understand Grantie all right. Is there anything more tempting than living through other people's approval? Or more futile?

'By the way,' said Steve. 'He asked me not to tell anyone about the steroids.'

'Oh, I won't . . .'

'But I told him it's bound to get out,' he added casually. 'Anyway, Andy's panting to use the phone. See you about half seven by the entrance, all right? And – oh yeah, I'm going to fix you up tonight.'

Before I could reply he'd rung off. Fix me up? How awful that sounded. And I've no intention of being fixed up. Even by Steve. My name is Rich now and that means I'm standing up for myself.

As I ran upstairs the phone rang again. Mum answered in her usual apprehensive voice while I waited, just in case it was, but no. I didn't think it would be.

I rang Ash on Sunday and Monday night. Both times I got her sister and both times she said Ash was in bed asleep, getting over a bad cold. And the second time she didn't actually say don't ring again but she went on about this mysterious family crisis and she seemed to imply that Ash had far more important things to do than talk to me. Perhaps Ash had told her to put me off. That thought stopped me ringing again.

I can stand anything but rejection.

Anyway, Ash certainly hasn't rung me – and no-one has seen her. She hasn't been at school all week. Although this afternoon Katie said she'd seen Ash sitting by herself in the library. Of course I zipped over, but she'd disappeared. Still, at least she is about and if she goes out anywhere tonight, there's a good chance it will be the fair.

And when I see her I'll go over to her with a big smile (though not so big I show off my fillings), and if she cuts me dead I'll be very cool and dignified about it. I hope.

I changed into my new clothes. The laugh is, I've been wearing some new clothes about the house so Mum can get used to them – and she really likes them – said they're 'tasteful' and nothing like what the punky hooligans wear.

Before I leave I put my head round the lounge door. A somewhat different scene to last Friday: Mum is knitting something very large and gloriously unidentifiable. Dad is stirring his tea. They look up anxiously at me, poor things. No doubt they are wondering what fresh trouble I'm going to throw at them.

Earlier this week I'd told them about my financial embarrassment: namely that I owe tons of money on the party and I've spent all my savings. They were all right about it, eventually. And Dad said he'd lend me the money to pay for the party on condition I only worked at Bunce's two nights a week. He thought working there every night was too much, considering all the homework I was doing. Neither of my parents knows how little school work I'd done for two months. I thought it was best to limit them to one shock a week.

Before I could tell them where I was going Mum said, 'That was your sister on the phone, she wants to see you next week.'

'Why?'

'Well,' said Mum coyly, 'isn't it natural for sisters to want to see their little brothers? She said you're to ring her and fix up a time when you and she can go out for a drink and she'll arrange with Justin to baby-sit that night.'

I couldn't hide my pleasure. 'Well yeah, I'll ring her, sure.'

'Kay said she hasn't had a good chat with you in ages – and she always so enjoys talking with you . . .'

'You off somewhere, son?' said Dad suddenly.

'Oh yes, Penn Fair. A friend's paying for me.'

'That's nice of her,' said Mum, assuming it was Ashley. 'But are you sure . . .'

'Have a good time,' said Dad, interrupting her. 'Do you good to stretch your legs a bit and it looks like it's going to be a nice evening. Don't leave it too late though getting back, will you?'

'Oh no, no. I should be back by eleven, probably earlier.'

'Have a good time then,' he said.

As I closed the lounge door I could hear frantic whispering and before I opened the front door Mum appeared, thrusting a ten pound note in my hand.

'Can't have you going out looking so smart with no money in your pocket. And besides, girls like it if you pay for a few things.'

'Thanks Mum,' I said, putting the tenner in the front part of my jeans.

At once Mum's hand started delving down my front pocket.

'Mum, what are you doing?' I gasped.

'Just stuffing it right down,' she said, 'the way you had it someone could have whipped that money out of your pocket, quick as lightning.'

With my ten pounds well and truly stuffed, I strolled around Penn Fair with Steve. It was one of the year's first warm evenings and teenagers were out in droves. And although the fair was quite a small, shabby affair – in fact some of the stalls were positively weedy – I enjoyed being there. And it was more than that too. Last Friday my little house had had to contain all the bottled-up energy of packs and packs of teenagers – no wonder I'd felt threatened. But now the energy's been uncorked where there's space and fresh air and things to do and I can let the energy flow through me, lifting me right up. And you know what? I believe I'm really lucky to be my age.

Until recently I never knew I was a teenager. I let school clamp me down, I kept all my power and energy and emotions shut tightly inside. I was Anaemic Man, living my life within the confines of a textbook – a condition known of course as boffinitis.

But now I've freed myself and I never want to go back. Oh, I know the attractions of being a boffin. Someone like Mouse can pole-vault over all the hassles and mistakes and pain of teenagerdom. He'll be safe – but at what a cost! Who wants to be middle-aged at fifteen? No, I want to be in touch with myself, know myself, and that includes my age: I'm a youth, fifteen, right on the edge of things.

Being on the edge isn't very comfortable. There's the altitude – that can get to you and make you do crazy weird things which even you don't understand. And it's pretty scary way up there – no wonder some teenagers can't take it – and throw themselves off. But isn't it also the most exciting spot in the world: with your whole life ahead of you, all as fresh and unspoilt as an early morning, all hidden beneath vast mists of hope? Yes, the view can be marvellous, especially if there's someone looking out on it with you.

My eyes roamed around the girls thronging past. I don't think a day's gone by when I haven't spent a large part of it looking for Ash. No wonder I'm becoming quite expert at it. Once or twice I thought I saw her but as soon as the girl drew nearer, Ash vanished.

Steve saw me and thought I was eyeing up the girls.

'Not anything decent about tonight,' he complained to me.

'Actually, I was looking for Ash,' I said.

He never answered me.

But then I saw Anna, arm in arm with a bloke, going into the ghost train. I glanced at Steve and knew he'd seen them too. For straightaway he said, 'Look at the ass on that one.'

The girl he pointed out didn't look any different from the ones he'd been complaining about. But now Steve was going to me, 'Here's your first lesson in pulling the birds,' and he charged over to this shooting gallery.

'Right, I'm aiming for that big teddy. Here goes.' He aimed, fired and scored, bullseye. 'How about that then?' said Steve, grinning all over his face. And even the stall-holder had to congratulate him on his shooting. Then Steve started running over to this girl whose ass he'd so admired. She was standing by the waltzers with another girl.

'Come on, Ricky, keep up.'

'It's Rich,' I said, chugging along behind him.

As we approached the girls Steve said to me in a loud voice, 'So what am I going to do with this teddy? It's no use to me.'

Both the girls were staring at us now. Steve strolled up to his quarry with one of his arms round his teddy, the other tucked into his belt.

'I don't suppose you could give a home to this bear?' he said.

The girl smiled.

'Because if you don't, I'm going to have to drown it,' he said.

'Aaah, you can't do that,' said the girl. 'All right, I'll take it.'

'I know he's going to a good home,' he patted the teddy on the head before handing it to her. 'You've saved a teddy's life, er . . .?' he paused questioningly.

'Julie – this is my friend Sandy.' She pointed to a girl with ginger hair who'd been watching Steve's performance with undisguised admiration.

'I'd like a teddy too,' Sandy said. 'I could give it a room all to itself too,' she added, 'during term time anyway, when my sister's away at uni.'

'All right, Sandy, I'll get you a teddy on my very next shot. Come and watch if you like.'

'May as well,' said Julie, slouching a few paces behind us. Sandy couldn't contain her enthusiasm quite so well.

As we went back to the shooting gallery Steve whispered to me, 'I don't know which one I want now. That Sandy's not bad either, is she? Who do you want?'

'As neither of those girls has looked at me for more than a millionth of a second I should think it highly unlikely I would get either one of them – even if I wanted them – which I don't. I hate picking up girls like this.'

'Prefer to meet them down the library, do you?' jeered Steve. 'No, I'll get you fixed up, it's time you were fixed up,' he added. 'People will think you're a bit funny if you don't get a girl on your arm soon.'

Then Steve darted a smile at the girls who were five paces behind us, whispering and plotting madly.

'My mate's just said you both look really horny. I told him not to be so cheeky.'

The girls tittered, Steve nudged me jubilantly while I went beetroot red. It was starting again. Steve was pushing me into things, telling me what I should be doing, worrying me. I'd stopped enjoying myself.

At the gallery Steve twirled his right hand in the air – he was wearing one of those gloves which are made of the same rubber spongy stuff as table tennis bats – and announced 'I will tell a joke and score a bullseye in twenty seconds. Right, this Irishman's got a load of horse manure in his hand. He goes, "Look what I nearly stepped on."'

Instantaneous with their laughter, Steve's shot was right on target. The stallholder was considerably less delighted this time, but the girls clapped their hands as Steve flourished another teddy bear in the air. He handed it to Sandy.

'Oh, how wonderful,' she cried, but she was looking at Steve – not the teddy.

Both she and Julie were waiting for him to make the next move.

But it was then Anna and her boyfriend happened past. Immediately Steve picked up the gun. 'Ignore her,' he hissed to me as he fired a whole barrage of shots – most of them now totally off target.

Anna saw me. I smiled. I thought it was totally kiddish to ignore her.

'Hello, Ricky,' she said, smiling triumphantly because she'd finally got my name right. I didn't like to tell her I'd moved on to a new name now. She put her hands up to her ears to block out the noise of Steve's shooting.

'Ricky, may I introduce Mark Bateman-Jones?'

I shook hands with a tall guy who looked about twenty-five. His hands were very sweaty.

'I am very pleased to meet you,' he said and then looked away, put his arm back behind Anna's shoulder, and they were about to move off when I said,

'You haven't seen Ash, have you?'

Anna looked surprised. 'Ash's gone,' she replied.

The words seemed to echo, bouncing off my ear-drum. 'Ash's gone, Ash's gone,' while my breath caught somewhere down in my chest.

'Where's she gone?' I gasped.

Anna, picking up the tremor in my voice, turned to her escort, 'Mark, go and win something edible,' she said airily, pointing to a hoopla stall. Mark took the hint.

Then she said gently, 'Let's go over here, away from that racket.'

Steve and the stallholder were now shouting at each other. I wanted to get away from that din too. So we stood by the most deserted stand at the fair, Madame Zena, the fortune-teller.

'I don't know much,' said Anna, 'only I rang Ash this evening and she sounded a bit strange, but friendly. She apologised for last Friday – and I said I was the one to apologise and suggested we go out for a drink. She said she'd like to but couldn't as she had to leave tonight.' Anna lowered her voice although there was no one within listening distance. 'She said something about her father leaving. I thought at first Ash was leaving with him. But it turns out,' her voice became ever lower, 'Ash's dad ran off with his secretary last Friday. Just before your party Ash found a note and some money from him. Now she doesn't even know where he is. He rang Ash – apparently from some secret love nest – saying he wouldn't be coming back. So for the last week Ash has been ill and staying home with her sister and live-in step-mother. It must have been awful. Anyway, both the sister and step-mother have cleared off now.' She paused, 'I really wanted to talk longer with Ash. I said to her couldn't we have a quick drink before she left. But she said she had all her packing to do and she had to be at Wycombe bus station for 9.49 or 9.29 this evening, something like that – her mum's meeting the bus in London – I think she said. Are you all right, Ricky? You've gone a deathly white.'

'Oh yes, I'm all right.'

'If only Mark had brought his car I'd get him to drive

you over to her house – and you might just catch her before she leaves.' She looked at her watch. 'But it's half past eight now. She might even be on her way already. I'm sure she will contact you when she's got herself sorted out though. You'd better sit down, you look distinctly groggy.'

'Did she say how long she'd be away?'

'No, with her father away she might – but I'm sure she'll ring you one day when . . . Oh no! Can't men do anything right?'

Mark Bateman-Jones was striding towards us, waving a tin of toffees. 'You got toffee,' Anna wailed at him. 'You know I can't eat toffees, they stick on my teeth. You can just take that back.'

Both Mark and his toffee box drooped before Anna's disapproving gaze. 'I don't think they'll take it back,' he said, 'I haven't got a receipt or anything.'

'I'd better go,' said Anna briskly, 'otherwise he'll bring something else I can't eat. Will you be all right?'

'Oh yes, fine.'

'I'm sure she'll ring you,' said Anna before she led Mark Bateman-Jones back to the hoopla stall.

It's got darker and colder. I've had enough of the fair. I'll find Steve and tell him I don't feel too good and I'm going home.

I shiver as I pass, the stalls: pathetic, burnt-out little stands, and I know what lies behind them – deep, unending blackness. That's what lies behind everything. The closer you peer the deeper the blackness. But you know what? I'm still looking for Ash. She's left – perhaps for good – without even saying goodbye and I'm still looking out for her.

It's very dark now. Through the blackness Steve's voice – still rowing.

'Look, you're saying I can't use this gun because I've won too many prizes. Admit it.'

'No, it's because your shooting is wild and dangerous.'

'Crap, you've . . .' and then he must have spotted me. 'Hey, Ricky, my main man,' he yells hoarsely.

'My name's Rich,' I mutter. No-one hears me.

Steve is shouting right in my ear. 'Okay then, I won't fire your gun, my mate will. Can't stop him, can you? All right, Ricky, you just follow my instructions and you'll win a nice prize for one of these young ladies . . .' He's going on and on. I don't get a chance to tell him I'm leaving. No energy left: Ash's gone. Ash's gone.

A gun flops into my hand. What's this for? I try to let go of it. Can't.

'Don't be silly,' says Steve, 'I'll help you.' Then he shouts, 'No, I won't fire it for him. I'm only helping him. Come on, Ricky. Now shut one eye.' I shut both eyes, bring on the blackness. More and more of it. But in the corner of my eye there's a kind of stirring, a light, very faint, very far away, struggling towards me . . .

'Now lay one cheek over the furniture – go on, like so.'

I wish he'd stop shouting. He frightened the light away. Now it's all black again. Ash's gone. Ash's gone. But there it is again, stronger, much stronger. A real shaft of light and a picture's trying to form, an idea's unfolding. Now I see . . .

'Pull the button to your shoulder and shoot when you've breathed all your air out.'

I'm touching an idea and Steve's trying to blow it away.

'Come on, do it. Do it.'

He's screaming in my ear, pulling me back into the darkness, forcing me . . .

'For God's sake fire, Ricky.'

But Ricky can't fire. Ricky's gone. I'm my own man now. I'm not under his charge any longer. I won't be pushed around any more.

In a fury I seize hold of the gun really tightly – 'That's it, Ricky' – and hurl it to the ground.

Steve lets out a startled cry of pain as if I've thrown it on his foot. I haven't – while I run towards my idea. I've got to get out of this fair and on to the Penn road. I run to the fair's entrance, crammed with new arrivals. Presumably the road round the fair must lead on to the Penn road. From there I can pick up a bus to . . .

But Steve's tearing after me, easily overtaking me!

'What the hell did you do that for?' he storms.

'I didn't want to fire the gun,' I say simply, almost sulkily, as if I'm talking to a teacher.

'Why in hell not?'

'I didn't want to. Just because you like firing guns doesn't mean I have to. I don't like doing all the same things as you. Is that so strange?'

Steve looks at me in angry puzzlement. 'What's with all the verbal? You tried to fire a gun and lost your bottle – okay, fair enough. Now be a man and try again.'

'Why should I?' I yell at him. 'So I can misshape myself into your image of a man? That's why you like helping me, isn't it? I won't do anything except the will of Steve. Well, I'm not ending up like Tim Grant.' I hadn't meant to say all that – but now it's said.

'You'd better watch yourself, mate,' he says, poking a fist at me. 'And you'd better explain exactly what you meant by that last crack. 'Cause if you're saying I'm responsible for Grantie taking those steroids I'll – I'll . . . First I knew of that was today – and what happened to Grantie is nothing to do with me, right?' His voice seems like the voice of someone arguing with himself.

'All right, Steve, I shouldn't have said that. I'm sorry but I really have to go now.'

'Running home to Mummy, are we?'

'No, Wycombe bus station.'

'What?'

'Ash is leaving from there tonight.'

'Why?'

'Oh, various problems, family ones mainly,' I say quickly.

'I suppose you blame me for her going too. Well, go on, I can take it!' he says, his voice cracking more.

'No, I didn't say that. It's only I have to rush because she's leaving just after nine. And I've got to pick up a bus on the Penn road.'

246

'How do you know she wants you there, waving her bye bye?'

'I don't. I just want to show her someone – someone's there for her . . . someone cares.'

Steve stares at me in undiluted disgust. 'Well, go on, clear off to her then. She made a right exhibition of herself last Friday but I suppose you thought I should have been out there holding her hand. Well, I didn't, and you know why? 'cause looney people scare me. And it seems to me I'm the only non-looney around here: first her wailing like a banshee in the rain, then Grantie . . .' He waves his hands as if he can't bear to repeat what Grantie's done. 'And now you turning flakey. You're all sick and make me sick.' There is a look of such terror on Steve's face it would be comic if it weren't so sad.

I don't want to argue with him – especially with time rushing by – so I just say quietly, 'I'm leaving now.' I like the way I say it, full of quiet dignity, and I even walk with very quiet dignity until Steve calls tauntingly, 'Why are you going in the wrong direction?'

I halt. 'Pardon?'

'I thought you were going to the Penn road?'

'Yes.'

'Well, you have to go back through the fair, on past the caravans and out through Wye field . . .'

'Ah,' I haven't a clue what he's talking about. With the greatest embarrassment I ask, 'Could you show me?'

'No.' Steve starts stomping away, then turns back.

'Oh, follow me, dillick-brain.' Then he whines to

himself, 'He hasn't a good word for me – but I'm still supposed to sort him out.'

I half-run alongside him, he's walking very fast, but his shoulders are stooped and his eyes seem to be sinking into his head.

To think this guy was my hero. I was right to have a go at him. He does bully people into doing what he wants and as for what he did to Ash, that was savage. No, he's just a big kid, living by a stupid code that he tries to inflict on suckers like me.

And yet, here he is pointing me on the right road. How many other times has he helped me, looked out for me, instructed me in teenage etiquette and wasn't it really Steve who first gave me the chance to be someone different? Without him . . . Why did he do it? Why did he help me? Because he's a bully and likes to impose his will on weaker people. Was that the reason? The only reason?

I'm about to run off. But I want to show Steve I know I owe him something. I can't think what to say, especially as he's just scowling down at his trainers. I start to walk away from him, when on impulse I turn back – he's still standing there, pretending not to watch me. 'Steve,' I call out. He looks up and I salute him.

'What the hell are you doing now?'

'Mark of respect to my former commanding officer.'

'Now I know you've cracked,' he mutters, then suddenly calls out, 'You never thought I helped you 'cause I enjoyed your company, did you? No, that's too simple for a boffin like you.'

He doesn't wait for the reply. Instead he starts stumbling back to the fair, moving more like an old man than Steve. But his last words keep racing through my head as I run down the field and hurl myself on to the Penn road. I speed towards a bus stop and to my amazement, a bus turns up two minutes later. I change Mum's tenner – it came in really useful after all – and sit watching some lads in front of me swaying and singing.

But they're quickly deafened by my own thoughts. Back at the fair I'd sensed Ashley needed someone . . . me. But it was just a feeling – this could be a wild goose chase.

And now I'm in a dark hole called Wycombe Bus Station. It's practically deserted except for what I suspect are its locals. Old guys huddled in the corner conversing through coughs – while another sits snoring over his pile of unsold papers. Skulking in the shadows a quartet of teenagers with sharp eyes and no doubt even sharper knives – they're waiting for something or – someone.

It is here I begin my last search for Ash.

Destiny and I Are Not Strangers

I feel rather silly. You see, I've no idea which bus Ash will be catching – and I'm too churned up to start translating bus timetables – so I'll just have to patrol this entire station.

I quickly rifle through a set of middle-aged women cackling with laughter. No, Ash certainly isn't with them. But looming alongside them is a double-decker bus: dark, driverless, yet showing definite stirrings of human life. I squint up at it. There's a girl upstairs. Can it be? I stand right next to the bus, gazing upwards. No, no, nothing like Ash.

I turn round. The women have stopped laughing and are staring at me in silence. They continue staring at me as I examine the contents of the single-decker bus alongside.

I proceed down the station, carefully inspecting each bus and picking up a fine collection of funny looks. No doubt some station official will be tapping me on the shoulder any minute and asking me why I'm behaving so suspiciously.

By now I'm right at the end – just one more bus to check. As I approach it a driver gets on – the only driver I've seen all night. The passengers step out of the darkness of the station into the darkness of the bus. Ash won't be on this one. Ash's gone . . . Ash's gone.

And right then the bus bursts into glowing light and I stare inside and there she is. There's Ash.

She's stumbling down the bus carrying a case which looks much too heavy for her. She leaves the case in the corridor, sits herself down, then starts hoisting the case alongside her.

I watched fascinated until I realise she'll be leaving very soon. I knock on the window at her. She looks up, blinking at me disbelievingly. Then she rushes down the bus and . . .

She's wearing hardly any make-up. She's got a grey coat on and looks so marvellous – nothing like my last glimpse of her – that I'm suddenly shy. It's as if a year has passed since I last saw her in my back garden, not one little week.

Then she says, 'I don't believe it.' while I reply, 'Nice to see you, Ash.' You'd think I'd just casually bumped into her. 'I wanted to say goodbye to you – and wish you all the best. Anna told me . . .'

Thankfully Ash interrupts me – as usual at times like this I'm talking utter rubbish – and says, 'You know I've been thinking about you so much this week, I feel as if I've suddenly conjured you up here.'

I stare at her doubtfully. Can I, in my fevered state, have misunderstood her? 'You've been thinking about me?' I say.

Ash nods excitedly, 'All day today I've been writing you a letter. And I hate writing letters normally. You ask any of my penfriends. But do you know how long your letter is? Eleven pages. There's just so much I wanted to tell you I couldn't stop. Mind you, I write like a worm and it probably won't make any sense.' Ash suddenly pushes me away from the bus, throbbing and wheezing behind us. 'Let's sit over here a second,' she says.

We sit down on a long hard seat opposite her bus. And Ash's smiling at me while I decide: I can't let her leave now. I can't.

'Did Anna tell you about my dad?'

'A bit.'

She nods. 'Poor Dad, he's going through a bad patch at the moment. It's Denise I feel really sorry for. You met her, didn't you?'

'Yes, I liked her.' I remember it was Ash's dad I hadn't liked.

'Denise left Wednesday. Same day as Jo, my older sister, who's been looking after me in her way. It was great having the house all to myself for a while – but there's a limit to how long you can play your hi-fi loud, isn't there?'

'So now you are going to stay with your mum – in London.'

Ash nods, 'She's meeting me off the bus. Her boyfriend's house is very near where the bus comes in and she said she hoped to be there to meet me, which'll be good.'

I get ready to insert my comments about why Ash shouldn't leave with friends like me here when she says, 'And Ricky, I've done something really different for me – that's what my letter to you's about really. You see I spent days just lying in bed feeling so miserable and low. I didn't have any energy for anything except feeling sorry for myself. And then I thought of you and of the amazing things you've achieved recently, how you've turned your life around.'

'Well, I . . .'

'Oh yes you have, you dared to be someone quite different. So I thought, why shouldn't I try something different too? So I have.

'You're looking at a designer,' she smiles at me triumphantly. 'Well, I don't expect I'll get that far. But you know I'm always drawing designs for dresses – you saw some once. Awful, they were. But anyway, I read about this course in London – not too far from Mum's house – all about costume design and jewellery – and the school has given me permission to go on it, probably glad to get rid of me. Anyway, I've written out all the details in your letter.'

She glances at the bus which is revving up.

'I'd better start talking fast – anyhow, Ricky, I thought why don't I at least try this course? I mean, I'll probably be awful but . . . but what do you think?'

How desperately I wanted to say to her, Don't go, don't

leave me, stay here – but also, I knew Ash was right to go on the course.

And I could only admire the way Ash was trying to make something good out of all the disasters which had befallen her lately. So I had no choice but to say, 'I think you're quite right to go, Ash. It's a great chance for you and – for them. You're going to be the world's greatest costume designer – at least!'

'Oh, I knew you'd support me,' she cries. 'My sister, of course, thinks I'm quite mad. But then I think she's mad. I mean, she's married to this guy she hardly knows – she had morning sickness on her wedding day – and he's giving her such a mean life. But she says that he's all she's got. And because he's good-looking – just like a guy out of a magazine – she thinks she won't get a better man than him.

'I'm all over Steve,' she added quickly. 'Like my sister my trouble is I read too many soppy stories. And Steve looked so like the dream man in the magazines, I made him into mine. But he isn't that person. He hasn't really got any of the qualities I gave him. I saw him today, you know. Oh, he didn't see me. I watched him through the library window and you know, he's not even that good-looking. I mean, he's got a really big nose. Funny, I never noticed that before.' She smiles nervously. 'In my letter I apologised for ruining your party.'

'You didn't ruin it.'

'I didn't help. And I felt so ashamed I dreaded facing you. I felt as if I'd let you down. Perhaps if I hadn't had that note from my dad the same day . . .'

'We're about to leave,' bellows a voice.

At once Ash and I run towards the bus, now chugging impatiently.

'You've come all this way,' says Ash, 'just for a minute of me gabbing away.'

'It's been worth it.'

'A few minutes later and you'd have missed me completely.'

'No,' I reply. 'I knew I'd see you.'

We're almost at the entrance now.

'How long will you be away?' I ask.

'I don't know,' says Ash. 'All my dad would say on the phone is that he'll keep in touch, so perhaps quite a long while.'

I shiver.

'But I'll give you a ring tomorrow,' she says. 'When will you be in?'

'All day,' I say promptly.

'And why don't you come up to London one Saturday, Ricky?'

'Yes,' I say, picturing the scene already. 'Yes, I'd like that – and my name's Rich now, by the way.'

She strokes my hair. 'I like to keep up to date with your names,' she says. 'Even though you change your name nearly as often as I change my hair colour! Well, Rich, Ricky, or whatever your next name is . . . I must go but thanks – thanks for so much.' She kisses me and for a moment I'm lost in her softness.

'Come on, let's be having you,' snarls the driver.

Ash grins apologetically, 'Such a nice turn of phrase that man's got.'

We're right by the steps. I start to edge away, 'Make sure you ring tomorrow!' I call. 'You've got my number?'

Ash nods and all of a sudden she's in my arms again whispering, 'By the way, just thought I'd tell you, I think you're a great person.'

'Finally got you fooled, have I?' I croak.

She smiles, 'No, no, I think I've got you just about right.' Then she boards the bus while I hover by the first step.

'You getting on too?' calls the driver.

'Er, no,' I mutter, embarrassed. 'No, not getting on.'

The bus door promptly wooshes shut. Then the bus steams its slow way out of the station. I stand, staring after the bus, long after it has gone.

I sit again, where I'd sat with Ash. In a minute I'd better find out what time my bus goes . . . in a minute.

I don't know how long I sat there. Quite a long time. Until I peer idly at the wall and see a ghost – faded now but I'd recognise it anywhere. Could I ever forget that fat whalelike body or that motif – SAVE THE BOF IN? Only an F is missing or rubbed out, not sure which. But there it is at the bus station, almost as if it's been waiting for me, knowing I'd end up here one day.

Poor Boffin. He wasn't all bad. He enjoyed books and was clever at school – so is that a crime? Not at all. And Boffin'll always be there, a part of me – I know that. Now I'm going to make full use of Boffin but because I want to, not because I'm scared of any old teacher.

But Boffin isn't all of me. I know that too. There's more to me than meets the eye. There's more to everyone than meets the eye. Like Steve. Every time I think I've got him nicely pigeonholed he says or does something . . . keeps changing. And now something's happened to me that's never happened before. All right, no girl fell into my arms, moaning, 'I love you.' All right, I'm going home alone and without Ash . . . But tonight she called me a great person – she's wrong of course – but I sure enjoyed hearing her saying it.

And when Ash sat on the bus just as it was leaving, she smiled at me. Only it wasn't her usual smile.

For when she smiled at me her face lit up and her eyes – there were candles behind her eyes.

So if that can happen today – who knows what lies ahead for me and for you? Anyhow, it's over to you. Your story. Perhaps you'll tell me your story one day – until then, here's to you and wishing you the best, always.

Psst!
What's happening?

sneakpreviews@puffin

For all the inside information on the hottest new books,

click on the Puffin

www.puffin.co.uk

hotnews@puffin

Hot off the press!

You'll find all the latest exclusive Puffin news here

Where's it happening?

Check out our author tours and events programme

Best-sellers

What's hot and what's not? Find out in our charts

E-mail updates

Sign up to receive all the latest news
straight to your e-mail box

Links to the coolest sites

Get connected to all the best author web sites

Book of the Month

Check out our recommended reads

www.puffin.co.uk

Read more in Puffin

For complete information about books available from Puffin – and Penguin – and how to order them, contact us at the appropriate address below. Please note that for copyright reasons the selection of books varies from country to country.

www.puffin.co.uk

In the United Kingdom: Please write to Dept EP, Penguin Books Ltd, Bath Road, Harmondsworth, West Drayton, Middlesex UB7 ODA

In the United States: Please write to Penguin Putnam Inc., P.O. Box 12289, Dept B, Newark, New Jersey 07101–5289 or call 1–800–788–6262

in Canada: Please write to Penguin Books Canada Ltd, 10 Alcorn Avenue, Suite 300, Toronto, Ontario M4V 3B2

In Australia: Please write to Penguin Books Australia Ltd, P.O. Box 257, Ringwood, Victoria 3134

In New Zealand: Please write to Penguin Books (NZ) Ltd, Private Bag 102902, North Shore Mail Centre, Auckland 10

In India: Please write to Penguin Books India Pvt Ltd, 11 Panscheel Shopping Centre, Panscheel Park, New Delhi 110 017

In the Netherlands: Please write to Penguin Books Netherlands bv, Postbus 3507, NL–1001 AH Amsterdam

In Germany: Please write to Penguin Books Deutschland GmbH, Metzlerstrasse 26, 60594 Frankfurt am Main

In Spain: Please write to Penguin Books S. A., Bravo Murillo 19, 1° B, 28015 Madrid

In Italy: Please write to Penguin Italia s.r.l., Via Felice Casati 20, I–20124 Milano

In France: Please write to Penguin France S. A., 17 rue Lejeune, F–31000 Toulouse

In Japan: Please write to Penguin Books Japan, Ishikiribashi Building, 2–5–4, Suido, Bunkyo-ku, Tokyo 112

In South Africa: Please write to Longman Penguin Southern Africa (Pty) Ltd, Private Bag X08, Bertsham 2013